AF589083

Praise for *Hot Water*

'A story that holds tenderness alongside all of life's sharp edges.'
—Deepa Anappara, author of *Djinn Patrol on the Purple Line* and *The Last of Earth*

'Moving and gentle in the way it's told, the voices in *Hot Water* orbit one another precariously, revealing a tender mess, and creating an intimate portrait of family life that's both heartbreaking and heartening.'
—Aravind Jayan, author of *Teen Couple Have Fun Outdoors*

'*Hot Water* is a complex family story, masterfully told. Striking the chords of the heart, Govil is a writer far beyond her years, daring to broach the most sensitive and taboo subjects with delicacy and depth, bringing light to the darkest corners of our humanness.'
—JJ Bola, author of *Refuge* and *The Selfless Act of Breathing*

'I can't remember the last book that gripped me with such intensity that I literally couldn't put it down. I read *Hot Water* in two sittings, stopping only because sleep finally beckoned. Bhavika Govil writes with remarkable clarity and beauty about the complexities and secrets at the heart of every family home. Over the course of one sultry summer, those secrets slowly surface, revealing their devastating impact on a family seen largely through the eyes of a young brother and sister. Their childlike perspectives compel the reader to look between the lines. Ashu and Mira live with Ma, who is one moment charming and affectionate, the next distant and hurtful. Ma is a wonderfully complex creation: her life has not been an easy one, and as the story unfolds, the reader comes to understand her more deeply. Fans of Northern Boy - and its equally eccentric matriarch - will devour this book. I reached the final pages with increasing sadness, reluctant to say goodbye to Ashu, Mira and the indefatigable Ma, all of whom stole a piece of my heart.'

—Iqbal Hussain, author of *Northern Boy*

'Told primarily in the voice of the precocious and sweet Mira, the nine year-old daughter of Leela and sister of 14 year-old Ashu, Bhavika Govil's *Hot Water* is a beautiful and soft examination of what happens when emotions, new, hidden and overwhelming jam the cogs that keep family life in motion. Set against the pulsing heat of a Delhi summer but dipping into past, this is a story that unfurls through the mouths of the siblings as they try to make sense of the lives they live and those they wish they could, whilst contending with the fluctuating emotions of their mother. Govil's debut offering announces her as a bold and lyrical voice; one that kept me captivated page and after page.'

—Onyi Nwabineli, author of *Someday, Maybe*

'Bhavika Govil uses imagination, insight and humour to craft a tender but unsettling family tale. A charming and confident debut that I enjoyed tremendously.'

—Amrita Mahale, author of *Milk Teeth* and *Real Life*

HOT WATER

BHAVIKA GOVIL

JACARANDA

This edition first published in Great Britain 2026
Jacaranda Books Art Music Ltd27 Old Gloucester Street, London
WC1N 3AX
www.jacarandabooksartmusic.co.uk

A CIP catalogue record for this book is available from the British Library

ISBN: 9781806750252
eISBN: 9781806750276
Cover Design: Christina Schweighardt
Typeset by Siliconchips Services Ltd, UK

To Mumma & Papa. Thank you. You were right—the words did flow.

'That's what careless words do. They make people love you a little less.'

—Arundhati Roy, *The God of Small Things*

'... time was not passing...
it was turning in a circle...'

—Gabriel García Márquez, *One Hundred Years of Solitude*

He and I were doomed from the start. It was as if he had no confidence in my ability to take care of him, to feed him, to keep him alive. One time, a few months after he was born, I woke up after he had been wailing all night. I was parched, desperate for a sip of water, but his cries kept rising in intensity. I got out of bed and hurried to him. Those days, I used to put a black dot on his forehead to ward off evil spirits, a nazar battu, a superstition I had inherited from my mother. It stared at me, this black dot, looking abnormally large and out of place. I grabbed his forehead and rubbed it off until all that remained was a smudge.

When I bent over his cot to get him, I found that he was suddenly impossible to lift. He was heavy, heavier than the books had said. Though I pulled and tugged, I couldn't pick him up. He kept resisting, I kept trying. I couldn't understand what was happening and I began crying too—my tears louder and more urgent than the baby's—which now sounded like nothing more than a muffle underwater. Only, I was swimming in the middle of the ocean and he was the pile of rocks my foot had got stuck under. He kept weighing me down to the floor, and no matter how much I kicked and screamed and wailed, I couldn't pull out my foot from under him, I couldn't let it loose, I couldn't kick off the ground and buoy myself up, I couldn't breathe.

PLUNGE

MIRA

When I asked Ma why volcanoes erupt, she told me they had a tummy ache and had to belch all the lava out, thick, hot and molten. When I asked her why trees grow, Ma said that they were in a race to touch the sky. When I asked her why it rains so heavily sometimes that the water goes drip-drip-drip from the ceiling onto the bunk bed, she said the clouds were like a faulty water tap which a plumber had turned on in anger. Then, today, when I asked Ma about her big black mole, she said it's a little creature on her face who sees everything we think and do.

Ma and I were sitting in the dentist's office. Ma had promised me that we were visiting only because of her wisdom tooth, and not because of a cavity that I had somehow got without even knowing. OK, Maaa, I said, I'll go. But really, even if I had said no, I think she would have taken me anyway. Being at the dentist's is a lot like being at school. You have to wait in class and hold your breath while the teacher calls out many names before yours for attendance. You know your turn is coming but you're still nervous because you need to speak up and enunciate like Mrs Dubey insists and say Yes! or Present! like your heart isn't going thump-thump inside. Maybe that's how Ma was feeling too because she cupped her jaw with one hand and was biting the nails of the other.

Ma doesn't like us to tell people that she has bad teeth. It's her secret. Ashu has secrets, too, like the fact that sometimes he tells Ma that he is going to tuition but really, he is off to Rahul's place for hours. *I* don't have cavities. But because I'm only eight, I don't have any secrets either.

The dentist's office was in a basement with no windows in it because if you could see outside, you would want to run away—no one likes dentists, that's the rule. Ma was now flipping through a big pile of magazines that was kept on the table. Ma loves reading. She reads fat books and thin books, the back of the hair-oil bottle, and she has to read lots of things for her work too. She also likes to read our report card, but I don't like to think about that. At the dentist's, every two minutes, Ma clicked her teeth as she read and went *Ssssssst*, shaking her head like she was disappointed with the writer. Then she picked up another magazine. Ma is disappointed a lot—she gives me and Ashu a Look when we do things she doesn't like, like when we ask the same questions over and over or try on her kajal or lipstick without asking.

When there were only two names left before her turn, Ma clutched a magazine with bright yellow borders and a picture of lions in the front and sat up straight.

I asked her, 'What are you reading, Ma? What's so exciting?'

But she ignored me.

When she was done, she set the magazine down and said, 'There's a tiger cub in the Sundarbans who ate his mother's posterior when they ran out of food. Can you imagine?'

When we went back home, Ma had a funny look on her face, maybe because of the injection in her teeth but probably because she was still disappointed. She pushed a large casserole of rice towards Ashu and me and said, 'Don't want the two of you eating my bum. Serve yourselves.'

Later, both Ashu and I climbed all over Ma and fought about who would get to put the medicine paint on her gums. They had swollen up a lot and looked pink and bright like the colour of pomegranates, which I liked. Ma's teeth are stubborn, and don't rattle and move like mine do, especially when I bite too hard into a toffee someone hands out at school for their birthday. When it was my turn after Ashu's, I ran my little finger over her gum, especially the area where a tooth was now missing. I spread the paint on it lightly and imagined wise thoughts sprouting from the area and going straight into her head.

That night, I dreamt about little tiger dentists who were fighting over who would get to remove Ma's wisdom tooth. Everything was bright white and yellow at the same time, like the headlights of a car but right inside Ma's mouth. At the end of the dream, Ashu jumped out of a kiddie tiger suit—with a zip and everything—and inched closer and closer towards Ma. He was just about to climb onto the chair and open his mouth and roar, but I woke up before anything could happen.

* * *

When Ma first said we would be learning to swim I made a fuss. I like saying the word fussssssssss until I run out of breath inside me to keep making the *suh* sound. But Ma doesn't like it when I make it—not the sound, the fuss. She says I look like a tiny baby wailing with its face scrunched up, and not like an eight-year-old girl. So, I've stopped. Plus, Ma said that we have-to-have-to do it. When she says 'have to' twice in a row, it means she's really serious.

I didn't want to go swimming because I don't like going to the club. I don't like the soggy fries we eat at the canteen that taste like they were made a million years ago. I'm scared of getting lost underwater, or not being able to see what's going on up in the world.

What if sea monsters come and tickle my feet? Worse, what if they come and pee on my toes? Most of all, I don't like the way people look at us. Ashu and Ma and me. Everywhere we go, but especially at the club, it feels like people are always looking at us.

The club is about ten minutes from our house. When I was smaller, I thought that the whole world lived around us: the school, Ma's library, Mrs Shome's house, the shop from which Ma buys milk bread, the gulmohar tree under which old aunties and uncles throw their hands up laughing, Ashu's best friend Rahul's house, and the club with the swimming pool. When people at school would say where they were from, I used to think they were making names of places up and I would laugh. But now that I'm eight, I know better.

Ma drives us around everywhere in our sun-yellow car, always cool as a cucumber, no matter how many people honk at her or hiss something to her. Sometimes, rickshaw uncles wearing brown T-shirts and taxi drivers stop right in front of our car and say ugly things to Ma. One time, an uncle in a long car rolled down black windows and shouted, 'Why bother? You people can't drive.' Ma simply stuck out her middle finger and increased the volume of whatever CD she had on—Simon & Garfunkel, The Cranberries, or U2, I don't remember—and sang along. I wondered what the man meant by 'you people.' Did he mean people who worked in offices and read big books? Or those who had mud-brown hair like Ma—with a mole on the left cheek and a wisdom tooth-shaped hole now covered with gum paint? Could they not drive? Ma explained that he meant people like her and me—women. People without any hanging bits down their front—'Well, *most* women don't. But that's a conversation for later.'

In our home, there are two women and one boy—Ashu—and that's how it'll always be. Lots of people sometimes still think that I look a little like a boy because Ma cuts my hair short. She puts a katori on top of my head and takes the scissors snip-snip-snip around until my hair falls down and the floor becomes black. Ma always buries her nose in my ear after cutting my hair and says I look like a sweet little mushroom cap. And although I used to like having my hair like that, this year I am going to grow my hair long until it reaches my waist nice and swishy. You bet I will.

On the first day, which was the last day of school before the summer holidays, Ma scooped us into the car straight from school to go to the club. Ashu was sitting in the front seat as always, which he says is his birthright because he came into the world first. He says this to me all the time—when he wanted the top bunk of the bed, when there was a last slice of chocolate-orange cake in the fridge, and now when he wants to sit in the front. The seat belt in Ma's car or any car is too large for him, and Ma always has to double-strap it around to keep him in place, so he doesn't fly across the car every time she brakes. I sat in the middle seat at the back, jutting my face between the two of them, so I wouldn't miss out on any part of the conversation. Ashu began to complain that I was breathing too closely into his ear, so I shifted to the right a little.

We were at the big signal where all the roads zigzag into each other and cause a jam. Around us were small cars and big cars, green-yellow autos and buses and rickshaws and scooters all choked up against each other. In front of us was a truck carrying lots and lots of pet chickens stuffed together in crates, and to our right there was a van with so many tiny Coca-Cola bottles at the back that I suddenly wanted to roll down the car window and reach my hands out to grab them. On both sides of the road, there were mithai shops and jewellery shops and stationery shops, shops selling clothes and books, and the shop where Ma goes every month and buys money. In front of the big shops were even smaller shops spilling out onto the road. These were run by bhaiyas and didis on cycle carts, who sold bananas and oranges and big red pomegranates and too-hot sweet potatoes dusted with masala powder and black salt that I love.

'How was your day?' Ma asked, and my mind began to race with ideas. Other people are allowed to say their day was fine, okay, horrible or really, really great. But not us. We have to describe our time in food.

'Nimbu-paani,' I said, slinking into the backseat a little as the car lurched. I was happy with my answer. 'It was like nimbu-paani.'

Sometimes when I have a boring day, which to me is the worst kind of day, when nothing exciting happens at all, I say that my day was jammy. Time stood still like a jar of jam: sticky and boring.

Ashu mumbled something lame about his day being like a sandwich, and he wiggled in his double-strapped seat to turn to look at me. 'Days can't be like lemonade, silly. Only solid food allowed,' he explained in an annoying voice, as though he were the inventor of all games in the universe. Or a game-show host. 'And the answer is'—I imagined his shaky voice booming into a microphone and the beating of drums—'wronggg.' Ma said it was because of the new club he's part of. Ashu's new halfway voice. Half-thin, half-thick. Half-weak, half-strong. A few months ago, Ashu joined something called the *Pew Burty Club*, and only he and other boys and girls his age can be a part of it. When you become a member, your voice changes and you become taller and get funny marks on your legs and face. I think you also have to go for meetings every week, but Ashu is too lazy to do that. I wanted to remind Ashu of his funny voice because it made his cheeks turn red, but instead, I said:

'They *can* be. It was a sweet-and-salty day. I got some marks back—but I also found a fifty-rupee note in my school shirt!'

Ashu raised his voice at me now. 'You mean *my* shirt. That was mine until you took it.' Ashu turned towards Ma. 'Mira took my money again.'

'Finders keepers, Ashu. Right, Ma?' I looked at her with a grin.

At school, all the kids have started saying a few phrases that you can use for anything, anytime. 'Finders keepers, losers weepers' is my favourite. You can say it when you find something nice on the school grounds or on the bus or inside an empty desk, and even if it isn't yours, everyone has to let you keep it. Other phrases that work almost always are:

1. All's fair in love and war
2. Same to you, back to you, no returns
3. I'm sorry

I nudged Ma again. 'Ma? Right?' Then I wriggled to the left side of the car and looked up. Electricity wires were crisscrossing each other like a game of tic-tac-toe in the sky. Tiny green parrots flew between them, and even though I couldn't hear them and could only hear the loud honking from the road, I was sure they were singing. On top of the shops were people's homes. Their windows were open, and they had hung their towels and bedsheets out to dry. I imagined who lived inside. Maybe there were other Mas with their own Miras and Ashus who watched TV at the wrong time of the day and made bad jokes and hugged each other too much until their Mas asked them to stop. Outside, the signal was turning green. The men who were selling books to the people inside cars shouted to each other and ran out of the way. And all the cars and scooters and autos started honking until it became so loud, I had to put my hand on my ears to keep the noise out.

The Ma in the car slid a pair of dark green sunglasses from the top of her head onto her nose and told Ashu to stop fidgeting. Then she glanced back at me and said, 'Don't think for a second I didn't hear the part where you got your marks back. But we'll get to that later. Right now, won't anyone ask about my day?'

As she began to drive again, Ashu and I blurted out the question at the same time until we sounded like two voices mumbling-jumbling on top of each other. Sometimes, Ashu and I fight to get Ma's attention like we're trying to get a stuffed toy with a claw at the video game parlour. We try and we try, but it's really hard, and often, in the end, no one wins.

'Well, my day was like condensed milk lazily dripping. Mrs Shome and I had breakfast, I went to the office, and then I took a short nap.' Ma turned the car to the left so fast that Ashu and I almost slid to the other side of our seats like we were spaghetti. 'And now,' Ma said. 'Who's ready to swim?'

Ma always gives the best answers although Ashu and I try to beat her at it. I think I'm better than Ashu even if he's five years older than me. Ma also thinks so, I know, because she makes sure she always says it.

* * *

There is a coach whose name no one knows. He sits in a small chair near the deep end of the swimming pool in maroon swimming trunks with a whistle slung round his neck that he blows no matter what people do. Walk, swim, jump, or even just stand still and stare directly into the sun—peep peep peep. I think he is really annoying, but Ashu says that maybe he does that because no one actually listens to him. The first day we went to the pool, we heard lots of kids and their Mas shouting to him and he kept looking left, right and centre like he didn't know what to do. Everyone was calling him Coach. Even the people he wasn't coaching. It's funny how some people are always known by what they do. I asked Ashu, 'Does a police officer's husband also call her Officer at home?'

I tugged at his sleeve as he looked around the pool distractedly. 'Hmm?'

I repeated the question.

'Or a shopkeeper's son call him Uncle?' he joined in.

'Or Ma's dentist's wife call him Doctor?'

Our answers got sillier and sillier.

'Imagine Mrs Dubey's mother calling her Ma'am too.'

'Oh, Ashu,' I said. 'Of course *mothers* won't call their kids by what they do. They'll call them by their name, that's the rule.'

'Who said?'

'I did! If you became a—astronaut, Ma wouldn't call you Mr Spaceman, right?'

'She could.' He shrugged.

'Ask her,' I nudged him. 'Just ask her.'

But Ashu didn't, knowing he would lose. He just said I was being stupid and left me to pout.

We were standing and staring at a large blue pool in which waves formed as people splashed in and out. It was hot and loud. The sun was coming right into my eyes, and everything smelt a little like the shampoo Ma bought from the corner shop at the end of the month. People around us were doing all sorts of funny things. A small boy stood in one corner of the pool, crying and holding on to a pool float. An aunty, Ma's age or so, ran on her toes from the changing room to the pool like a thief, and right before jumping in looked around and tossed a bright blue towel to the side. And then there was us. Ashu and me, standing side by side—sweaty, sticky and fresh out of giggles. I scratched my hand even though there was nothing itching me, and I held Ashu's palm to my right and my watermelon-shaped swimming bag to the left. Ashu's hand was warm and clammy, and I had to rub it on my dress twice to remove the beads of sweat.

Ma pushed her green glasses to the top of her head and walked ahead towards the coach. When she held out her hand and called him Coach too, I didn't think it was so funny anymore.

The man fumbled for a moment, then got up. His whistle was swinging like a pendulum around his neck, right-left right-left.

'Ye-es,' he said, looking at Ma.

'Are you open for lessons?' Ma asked him a second time.

He nodded, then shouted at two other men with whistles who were talking to each other behind him to stop making noise.

'Yes, ma'am.' He shrugged like he were saying sorry, but I couldn't tell for what. 'You were saying? Classes? You want?' He looked past the big wart on his face at Ma from up to down. Then he stretched his arm out towards her.

Ma shook his hand and laughed a little like she usually does when she reads something funny. 'Nah. Not for me, Coach. These ones though,' she shook her head towards us, 'could do with some life-skill learning.'

'Yes-yes. It's important at their age,' he smiled, baring his lemon-yellow teeth at me and Ashu. 'Right, kids?'

Ashu stared at him with his eyebrows raised and didn't say anything. Most people don't know this about Ashu, but he is really good at looking scary without saying anything. I tried to follow him, staring at the man as hard as I could without blinking. Coach laughed nervously and looked back towards Ma.

'So, I'll leave them in your care then?' Ma shifted her weight from one leg to the other. I couldn't tell if she was bored by the conversation or just the opposite.

'Sure, ma'am. Just fill up the, uh, form at the reception, and bring the kids every Tuesday, Thursday, Saturday.'

'Got it,' Ma said. 'I trust you'll take care of them?'

'Of course, ma'am. Top-class coaches we have.'

'But you're the main one, Coach? You'll teach them?' Ma gave him a look I hadn't seen before, and Coach nodded quickly.

He also coughed and added, 'Ma'am, we have classes in the morning for adults also. Ladies, like yourself? Unless your husband minds—' He began searching behind Ma as if there were another person hiding there.

Ma shook her face fast-fast like she were swatting a mosquito off her cheek. 'No husband.' Then she put her hand on Coach's arm for just one second and said, 'But, flattered, Coach. I'll think about it.'

As she did this, something in my stomach felt tight. Ma dropped her hand from his arm and nodded. I left Ashu's side and quickly ran to Ma and held her hand, making it mine again.

* * *

On most days, Ma drives us to the club. After she fights with another member for a spot and parks the car, we walk past the badminton court and the café with tiny sandwiches, past the reading library and past the room where old people wrinkle their noses at playing cards and throw them down angrily when they lose. When we reach the pool area, we change into our costumes, and Ma sits somewhere in the corner to hide from the sun and watch over us while we swim. Honestly, though, most of the time, Ma is looking around at everyone else but me and Ashu, and I have to call out Maaa! Look! again and again to show her a new move I've learnt. I've decided that I don't hate the pool anymore. Turns out the sea monster thing was just a joke. Sea monsters can't make it to a pool—it's too far!

When Ma is busy or has a headache, she asks Mrs Shome to take us and we ride to the club in her car with the window down, letting the evening wind tie knots in our hair, and the bumps on the road make bruises on our bums. Sometimes, if we are too early for class, Mrs Shome lets us stop at a shop and pick up butter biscuits or momos from the street with a spicy-sweet sauce even though there is a no-eating-before-swimming rule. She says it doesn't really matter, and is just a silly rule made up by grown-ups for no reason. And even though Mrs Shome, just like Ma, sits close to the pool and reads whatever book she gets from home, I have a feeling that she is always looking out for us.

If we go in the mornings, it's a little cold in the pool at first, and our teeth chatter and make noises when we go in. Usually, after a while, we forget about it. But in the afternoons, the water is hot. Sometimes Rahul also comes to swim with us, but he is an advanced swimmer, and I know this because he keeps talking about it. He can already breathe underwater like a goldfish and do summer-saults in the pool. I asked Ashu if they're called winter-saults in December, and he just laughed. Rahul can also do this thing where he jumps in and stays underwater for as long as we count. When we're tired of counting, we give him a little tap under the water, and he pops right up. Because he doesn't need to learn swimming like we do and is there just for fun, sometimes he floats towards us in the middle of a lesson to talk to Ashu or to kick his legs up in the air or something and then floats back away.

Coach always walks around, a blur in maroon, and whistles all the time while saying things like: *Jump in, you girl* or *One, two, three* or *Paddle harder, faster, harder*. When he says these things, Ashu and Rahul put their hands up to their mouths and snicker loudly. I keep asking them what the joke is, but they just look at each other with a glint in their eyes and scoff at me. It's a teenager thing, they say. Then they splash water at me. I've decided: When I become a teenager in a few years, I won't tell them my jokes either.

Ma carries this small yellow-coloured tube that looks like a banana and squeezes out thick sunscreen tap-tap-tap onto her palm and onto us before we go inside the pool. She smears my arms and my cheeks and my neck in dots, and I have to guess what she is drawing on my skin. Today, Ma went round and round on my back, and I guessed it was a jalebi, which is my favourite sweet in the world. It wasn't. 'A mosquito coil? A snail?'

'You got it,' said Ma.

'Which one? Which one, Ma?'

'Hmm.' She was looking somewhere else as she answered. 'Oh, the coil. Good job.'

When I reminded her that she forgot Ashu, Ma pulled him towards her and covered his arms with so much paste that he looked like a ghost and I wanted to giggle.

'Ma, do I have to?' Ashu said sheepishly. 'I look—ugly.'

'On the contrary,' said Ma, continuing to lather on the cream. 'The sunscreen is a major improvement.'

Ashu huffed and mumbled something under his breath. Rahul was hanging around us too, but he didn't look like he had got any sunscreen on him at all.

Then, Ma put her sunglasses on and sat down on a lounge chair that looked like a bed. I once tried Ma's sunglasses, but they were too big for me, and everything became so dark and black that I couldn't see anything—not even my hands!

Rahul jumped into the pool headfirst, while Ashu and I walked down the steps to the shallow end. Coach came up to Ma. He was probably telling Ma some jokes because she laughed. Or maybe he was talking about us. I turned to discuss this with Ashu, but he was too busy talking to Rahul. Rahul is the same age as Ashu, though he is much, much bigger. Everything about him is a bit bigger. His laugh, his teeth, his hair, and even his swimming trunks that go down to his knees.

They were discussing who could stay underwater the longest.

'I bet it's me,' Ashu said.

When Rahul asked Ashu if he could prove it, Ashu laughed nervously and splashed water at him.

I kept looking at the two of them. I wondered why Ashu was showing off and telling lies. Ashu doesn't really like being underwater, not even for a minute, not at all. Besides, why weren't they asking me?

'I can.' I stuck my chin out.

Both of them laughed this time.

'Really, I've been practising!'

Ashu and Rahul first looked at each other, then searched to see if Coach was around. He was still talking to Ma. How long could this joke be?

'Okay,' Ashu agreed after a minute of thinking. 'You can try to hold your breath underwater for a few seconds.'

I said I could do that. I'd been practising under the tap at home. Glug glug. I made a fishy face. 'See?'

They grinned.

'Alright,' Rahul said. 'On our count.'

'And come up when you feel like you can't breathe, Mira, okay?' Ashu held my hand for one second then let it go.

I nodded earnestly, even though my heart was doing a little dance in my chest.

'One—two—thr—'

I bent my knees and dunked my head under the water, and sat cross-legged on the floor of the pool. I decided I would not get up from there until I reached a minute at least. That would show them, I thought, that I could join their games. I saw so many legs—jumping, splashing, dark legs, light legs, hairy legs, Ashu's legs—long like toothpicks, straight and awkward; Rahul's thick ankles, too, which were now kicking Ashu. Above the water was the sun, which was reaching my toes in little squiggly lines, and I felt cool liquid all around me. Above the water was also Ma, her eyes probably squinted, laughing. Green sunglasses. Maroon swimming shorts and a whistle.

I could hear almost everything going on above me, but it sounded wavy. Like when you put your head on the desk in the classroom, and you hear voices travelling through the wood and floating into your ear.

It was getting harder to hold my breath. But I had to keep counting. I opened my eyes wider and focused on noticing things nearby. Bits of hair floating around, a few coins with which I would buy ice cream if only I could reach them, and a fat yellow bee. The bee was drifting down towards the pool floor in crazy circles. Can bees swim? Was the bee dead? I gulped a little pool water as I tried to hold it in my hands to check, but it kept floating away. I followed it, kicking my legs wildly towards it, but the closer I got to the bee, the more it kept going to the deep end. I realised that I was also going towards the deep. No ground. No coins.

Water quickly entered my nose and my mouth, and I was gulping it now, like one glass at a time, trying to breathe. It tasted like soap and stung my throat. I began to cough when suddenly, I felt someone's hands on me, and I was jerked out of the water.

Air.

'She's okay!'

It was Coach. He'd held me under my arms and lifted me out of the pool. Ma was standing with him, and she pulled me into a tight hug that almost choked me. I coughed and she thumped my back one-two-three.

Both Ashu and Rahul loitered behind Ma.

'Why didn't you come up, idiot?' Ashu hissed at me, looking worried. Rahul was standing beside him, eyes down. Suddenly, he looked much smaller than before.

I gasped. 'I'm—I'm a fish, too.'

'What the hell happened?' Ma turned to shake Ashu's shoulders which trembled like a plate of jelly.

'We—we were playing a game—you have to hold your breath underwa—'

'I've told you before,' Ma hissed, 'to look after your sister.' Then she flung her hand out and slapped him across the face. 'Haven't I?'

ASHU

When Ashu lost his breath in front of people for the first time, he was nine. He had been on the school bus on a field trip to the fossil museum. He was sitting by the window, watching the roads twist and houses turn into trees. There was a small brown spider—about the size of his littlest nail—also riding on the bus with him. Ashu was counting the number of furry legs it had when the bus suddenly lurched to avoid a speeding truck. The boy to his right fell onto Ashu, pushing him against the windowpane. For a moment, the pressure was so immense, it was as though his bones were being crushed. Ashu dug his fingernails into the tearing rexine of the seat in front of him, feeling the air collapse around him, until it all turned black.

When his breath returned and Ashu opened his eyes, everyone was looking at him. His teachers took him aside when they reached the museum and asked him what had happened and why, what the last thing he ate was and when. He answered their questions quietly, pretended that he wasn't, in fact, regularly visited by a feeling of breathlessness, a tightness in his chest, this closing in of tall trees around him. He acted like he didn't feel the air escape his lungs whenever he was in a small room, a narrow corridor, on Mira's bottom bunk with his head too close to the ceiling, sometimes even when he was hugged by his sister too tight.

Eventually, he was checked, prodded, turned upside down. When nothing was found to be wrong with him, Ashu was put on an empty bus and returned home, slightly worse for the wear, where he sat on the steps outside his house until Ma came home. He mentioned nothing of it to her, partly because he didn't want to worry her. Besides, there was so much that she was already mad at him for, even though he was never sure why. He didn't want to add anything else to that list, so he crumpled the note from his teacher and threw it away.

A few days after the incident on the bus, Ashu reached school to find that their teacher, Mrs Dubey, was not in class. Instead, a mild-mannered, thin woman with spectacles stood with her hands on the desk. Every once in a while, she lightly hammered the chalkboard duster on her table, but to no effect. The fourth-graders could tell that this person had no real authority, and so the class was in a state of chaos. The students were shouting, yelping, making indiscreet sounds. They had removed the ties that went up to the nape of their necks and made them itch. Ashu entered the room and observed the mayhem. He scratched his leg with his shoe and walked quietly to the seat he always occupied—by the window, three rows from the front of the class. While the other boys had scrambled to sit next to the prettiest girls in the class, even fought with each other to find the best seats, Ashu preferred being loyal to his usual spot. The bell rang, and the last person to enter the class was the same tall boy who had fallen onto him in the bus. The boy usually sat in the last row, and he groaned loudly when he saw that the best seats had already been taken. Finally, he spotted an empty seat and walked over to Ashu. They talked for the rest of the day.

Ashu and Rahul's friendship began like this. Like most childhood friendships, it simply happened. They could have just as easily become friends any other way—while sharpening their pencils over the classroom bin, or walking in the same direction on their way home, or bumping into each other while filling their water bottles by the cooler, or getting placed in the same group project by a physics teacher. Or they could just as easily not have become friends at all.

At fourteen now, Ashu didn't think about that day on the school bus often, nor did he remember how Rahul and he became friends. But snatches of both came to him in his dreams sometimes—a mustard yellow school bus, a never-ending teacher's note that scrolled down all the way to his knees, a duster which floated in water—things that seemed so familiar, but garbled, like his own reflection in a funhouse mirror, and when he woke up he didn't quite know what to make of them.

Ashu wasn't unfamiliar to strange dreams. He had always had long, senseless dreams through the night, ever since he was a little boy. Once, he had dreamt that he was going to school in a large, outstretched limousine even though he'd only ever seen one on TV. He was sitting in it alone, with no Ma and no Mira, but there was a man that he'd never seen before in the front seat. Even though Ashu tried to look at him, wave at him, talk to him, the man ignored Ashu and continued to drive.

Other people visited him in his dreams too. Faceless women wearing bangles jingled their hands across his face and he laughed, endlessly, gurgling from the bottom of his stomach, the way you only do when you're a child.

Sometimes, when he dreamt, goosebumps, small and hard like tiny moons in the sky, appeared all over his body. He shivered, pulling his blanket closer and closer to his face, curling until he transformed into a tiny ball. When Ashu would wake up after such a dream, he'd notice that Mira would often ask him unusual things.

When he'd have a sad dream, one that made him feel small, Ashu would wake up to find her cuddling up to him. Once, he had a dream in which he flew through a waterfall and got drenched. In the morning, Mira handed him a towel. He looked at her strangely, wondering how it was that she was as much a spectator to his dreams as he was, how she knew.

There were times when reality filtered into his dreams. Like the first time he tried a cigarette. It was a little before the summer holidays had begun, and Ashu had thought it was a joke. The boys stood in a circle near the bus stand, feeling the sun's warmth on the back of their school shirts. Then Ishan, the most popular of them, took out a crushed white stick from his pocket. He held it up in the centre for all to see, and everyone, even Ashu, boisterously patted the boy on his shoulder and slapped him on his back to praise him. Though he would forget about this detail later, Ashu thought it was a stub of chalk at first, and he peered at it closer when someone said, 'Let's smoke it.' Ashu shifted on his feet and ruffled his hair, and a few flakes of dandruff fell to his shoulders. He gave Rahul a quick glance, and Rahul caught his eye and grinned. Ishan also pulled out a blue plastic lighter with a string attached to it. The lighter was smudged with fingerprints. 'Stole it from the shop.' Ishan smirked.

When they clicked the switch on and a little ball of fire began dancing at the tip of this lighter, Ashu didn't know what would happen. That in a few seconds, when the cigarette would be passed to him, he would hold it carefully between his Fevicol-stained fingers with the fire and ash staring him in the eyes. That Rahul would gently pivot the cigarette the right way around and Ashu would laugh nervously and say *thanks* under his breath. That while everyone would look at him and chant *go on, do it* he would lower his neck, feel the paper touch his lips and breathe in gingerly, like all first-time smokers do, his throat burning like sandpaper. That he would cough, feeling the sting in his eyes, and pass the cigarette to the person on his left. And later at home, he would run into the washroom and rub and rub his fingers with soap to get rid of the unmistakable smell.

That night, he'd have a dream about it. But this dream would focus on Rahul. It would focus on Rahul's fingers and Rahul's hair and Rahul's neck. When Ashu would get up the next morning, he'd sweat, burning in the summer heat. And for the first time after waking up, he'd turn away from Mira and walk straight out of the room in case she saw the things he felt in his dream; the things he thought; the things he didn't want anyone, least of all her, to know.

MIRA

'Did you know,' I began. 'Did you know that pools have more pee in them than water? Really. Everyone does it in swimming pools. Warm, sticky pee. Rahul once told me.' Ashu and I were sitting in the living room and waiting for Ma to get ready.

Ashu hadn't spoken to me for almost a whole day. I really wanted him to say something. Maybe tell me that he already knew about the pee thing or get bugged and ask me to stop making things up. We fight a lot—Ashu and me. We fight about who ate the last jalebi and who got hold of the TV remote and sometimes, Ashu fights with me when I listen to him talking on the phone. But honestly, most of the time, because we go to school together the next day, we forget that we had ever fought in the first place. It's only hours after we come back home that we realise we aren't supposed to be talking to each other at all.

But this time, we didn't have anywhere to go and forget. So, we just didn't talk. Ashu was mad at me because I made him let me play the pool game and he was mad at Ma because Ma hit him hard and Ma was mad at both of us because she was disappointed, and it was just a whole lot of mad in one single house.

That day, after we had got out of the pool, Ma wrapped me in my stripy pink towel, picked me up even though I'm too tall to be picked up and took us straight to the car. No shower. Throughout the car ride, especially after we'd dropped Rahul to his house, Ma gave us the Silent Treatment. The Silent Treatment sounds scary like a painful injection given by the doctor, but it isn't anything like that. It's when Ma says nothing, does nothing, hears nothing. She plays pretend that we aren't even there. One time, when I was smaller and Ma gave us the Treatment, I thought I'd turned into a small ghost like Casper and no one could see me. I worked on troubling Ma like a ghost would.

Ghost me: Helllloooo Maaaa

Ma: —

Ghost me: I'm sticking my fingers in my nooooose

Ma: —

Ghost me: I'm eating my own hairrrrr

Ma: —

Later, I began worrying that Ma really couldn't see me and I would get stuck this way forever. It was Ashu who spoke to me first and said that Ma was only joking. But if she was, then why was no one laughing?

This time, too, we stayed like that all evening, Ashu and me, patients of the Silent Treatment. Ashu hardly ate any dinner, and he even went to bed early which he hates to do. At night, when he was asleep, I took one step at a time up the ladder to his top bunk, careful not to wake him. I double-checked that he was snoring and not pretend-asleep and then I whispered 'I'm sorry' into his ear. I hoped he would have a dream that he forgave me and that when we woke up everything would be back to normal. But I must not have said it loud enough because in the morning, he still looked angry and was as quiet as ever.

Ma finally started talking to me when I went to wish her a good morning. She warned me to be more careful next time and gave me a kiss right in the centre of my ear, and I had to say Maaa stop, your kiss is so loud! I was feeling happy, especially because there was one less person mad at me, but I was still thinking about three questions from the previous day.

Question no. 1: Why did Ma slap Ashu?

Question no. 2: What joke was Coach telling Ma near the pool?

Question no. 3: I won the underwater game, didn't I?

But I didn't want to make Ma stop the kissing, so I didn't ask.

Later in the day, I thought of Question no. 4. I was in Ma's room and sitting on top of four pillows in the centre of the bed like it was a throne. Ma had small black splotches on her face that kept moving from the centre of her nose to her eyes to her cheeks because she was standing in front of a mirror with small black splotches on it. She looked a little funny because she had opened her mouth into a big O and was combing her eyelashes with a tiny brush.

'What?' Ma said, but because her mouth was open it sounded more like 'Ach?'

'Ma, do you love me more than you love Ashu?'

Ma now ran a bigger brush through her hair and said I was being foolish. She didn't sound like she was really listening to me.

'It wasn't his fault—'

'I'll be going out for a bit today.'

'Really. I wanted to try to stay underwater. I promised I—'

'I'll drop you at Mrs Shome's.' Ma continued as if she couldn't hear me. 'Behave well. She's being nice to babysit you.' She smacked her lips. 'The both of you.'

Even though I know what it really is, when I hear the word 'babysitting,' I think of big fat adults sitting on top of a sofa made of babies, the chubby baby faces bulging and their brown eyes popping out like pomegranates. I told Ma that.

She laughed. 'You're a morbid kid, aren't you?'

'Mawbid?'

'M-o-r-bid.' Ma was applying a swipe of lipstick on her lips. A bright red colour. She clasped the cap shut.

I knew not to ask Ma the meaning of the word. She always tells me to check it in the dictionary. She was telling me to do that even before I knew how to read.

'Okayyyy.' I stretched my legs out on the bed. Then I wondered that if Ashu and Mrs Shome and I were all going to be together, who was Ma going to be with? 'Ma,' I called out. 'Where are you going?'

'Oh. You know your Coach?' She said this with a weird glint in her eye. 'We're going to get a bite and discuss your swimming lessons.'

My stomach tightened. Coach? What did they want to talk about? Maybe he was going to tell Ma that Ashu and I were terrible at swimming. The swimming pool is kind of fun, but it's also where bees die and Ma slaps Ashu and I forget to breathe. So I wouldn't have a problem if Coach told Ma that we couldn't come to class. I wouldn't have a problem with that at all.

Ma says that Mrs Shome is the only one with half a brain in her office, besides herself. She is kidding. I've looked at Mrs Shome's head and it looks full from both sides. Mrs Shome must be older than Ma because she has a few grey hairs. She wears a big red bindi in the centre of the forehead that looks like the sun on a hot day. And she always talks in a soft voice. Both Ashu and I love her. Ashu does because she doesn't speak to us like we are kids who don't know anything. I do because she always smells like she's just baked something yummy and she uses difficult words that I don't know.

They both work in the admin department in their office and eat lunch together. An admin department has people who help make the ads we see on TV when they try to sell us things. Admin people know how to read your mind because whenever I wish for something, I see an ad for that on our TV. Like when I had a cold and my nose was leaky and going drip-drip everywhere, there was an ad for a magic balm to spread on your nose. And one afternoon when I really wanted to eat something sweet but Ma said no, there was an ad for the five-rupee Dairy Milk on TV that looked so good I wished I could put my hand through the TV screen and grab the chocolate. Sometimes I'm afraid that I'll think something bad like wanting a sister or a different brother—someone less like a game host and someone not a member of the Pew Burty Club—and there will be an ad for that on TV and Ashu will find out.

Mrs Shome's name looks like it rhymes with home, but Ma said her name is 'Shom-ay'. In my head, sometimes, I say Mrs Shom-hey! when I talk to her, even if she doesn't get to know. When Ma has-to-has-to go out for a long time, she leaves us at Mrs Shome's house even though Ashu says he's too old for babysitting.

Mrs Shome lives all by herself. Everyone says that people who live alone must be sad, but I have never ever seen Mrs Shome cry. Anyway, Mrs Shome didn't always live alone. She used to have a lot of people in her house once upon a time, but they all started leaving one by one when they grew up. 'Leaving to go where?' I asked Ma when she told us once, but she said that I was asking too many questions. Ma doesn't like us talking about people's families, not even our own, so we never do. One time, during babysitting, Ashu and I saw a photo frame of a younger Mrs Shome with a man and lots of children, but I think she saw us looking at it because the next time we went back to her house, it wasn't there.

Mrs Shome stays on the fifth floor of an old building without a lift, so while we're climbing up to her place, we usually sing the words to a song, one word for each step. Ashu and I like to take turns with the words. Like *Here's. To. You. Mrs. Robinson. Jesus. Loves.*

You. More. Than. You. Will. Know. Whoa. Whoa. Whoa. And. Hello! Mrs. Robinson. We. Are. Both. On. The. Fifth. Floor. Now. Hey. Hey. Hey.

Hey hey hey.

But that day, Ashu and I didn't sing at all.

When Mrs Shome opened the door, she gave me and Ashu one quick hug each before sending us inside. She and Ma stood at the entrance and spoke to each other for a while about things like work and life, and then Ma said Thank you so much, Anita and I'll be back in a couple of hours max, and Mrs Shome said Sure, no problem, best of luck!

But Ma wasn't taking an exam, I thought. What did she need luck for? Just before leaving, Ma came inside Mrs Shome's home for a second. She looked towards Ashu, who'd hung his head down, then came close to kiss me on the forehead. 'See you soon, sweetie,' she said, and she was gone.

A long, long time ago, when I was five and Ma would have to go out, she would start playing a game of hide-and-seek with me and then slip out of the house without saying bye. She used to ask Ashu to distract me because she thought I would cry and cry the way I did on my first day of school. She didn't know that actually I cried a lot more when she left in the middle of the game without saying anything to me at all.

Mrs Shome closed the door behind her with a soft thwack. Her house is many times bigger than ours even though she is the only one who lives there. She needs extra rooms for all her books and art because she reads and paints so much and they don't fit anywhere else. I've seen Mrs Shome's bookshelf, and it's even bigger than Ma's and has many books in languages I can't recognise. When I grow up, I also want a bedroom for my books and a different room for all my toys and one room full of bunk beds so I can make sure I get the top bunk every night.

'Can you get me some water, love?' Mrs Shome turned to

me now. Ashu was dragging his feet towards the sofa like he was moving in slow motion. I tried not to bump into him on my way to the kitchen.

When I came back with the water, Mrs Shome gulped it and set the glass down on the table with an *ah* sound like in those Pepsi-Cola ads on TV. No matter what we do, even if it's the smallest thing in the world, Mrs Shome always makes us feel like we have done something special.

Ashu, who had been sitting quietly till now and taking some of his things out of his backpack, rolled his eyes. 'It's just water.'

Mrs Shome looked towards him, narrowing her eyes like she was trying to see him better. It was only after a little while that she asked, 'So, Ashu, what have you got there?'

Ashu scrunched his shoulders up like someone had attached puppet strings to them. He turned a scrapbook towards her. He had been pasting some photos into it for holiday homework.

'Ah. So, you're covering Shakespeare! That looks quite fun,' she said. Ashu continued slapping things onto his scrapbook loudly. I could see that Mrs Shome was stopping a smile from coming to her face.

'It's, like, the opposite of fun,' Ashu mumbled.

'Are you looking forward to going back to school?' Mrs Shome continued, acting as if she couldn't hear what Ashu had said.

'No way! He hates school,' I replied.

She nodded and said to Ashu, 'What about your friends? Maybe you're missing them?'

I wanted to say that Ashu doesn't have many friends except for Rahul and me, but whenever I say that, Ashu says that I'm not his friend, I'm only his pesky little sister.

Ashu shook his head and said quietly, 'I got into a fight.'

Mrs Shome sat closer to Ashu to hear him. She asked, 'Who did you box up, tough man?'

Ashu could never hit anyone, let alone box them up. I started to giggle, but when I saw Ashu's face, I stopped.

'Had a fight with Ma,' he croaked in his new voice and then said something quickly under his breath about the pool and me.

I jumped in. 'Really, it was my fault. I wanted to hold my breath in the water for too long, and then Ma came, and there was a bee, and then Ma slapped Ashu.'

Mrs Shome tucked her hair behind her ears, and suddenly she looked to me a little like a cat with bright brown eyes. She said softly to Ashu, 'I hope you know that adults aren't always right.'

Ashu kept his book down on his lap. 'Whaddyou mean?' he said, mumbling-jumbling the words in his mouth.

'Adults can make mistakes too. Sometimes, their judgement is clouded, sometimes, they—they do things they shouldn't. And then maybe, they regret things later, but they can be too afraid to say sorry.'

'That's not fair. Everyone should be able to say sorry,' Ashu said.

'They should,' she nodded. 'But people rarely do.'

'Especially grown-ups,' I said firmly. I wanted Ashu to know I was on his side.

Mrs Shome smiled. 'Don't let us get you down, Ashu. You're a good boy, okay?'

'I thought I was a tough man,' Ashu grinned now, showing two of his teeth.

'You're a good boy and a tough man and everything else you want to be.' She ran her hand through his hair. Then she walked over to the dining table and opened up a box. 'Oh, did I mention? I have some extra gulab jamun that I made earlier. It's quite good, if I may say so myself. There's also some ice cream in the fridge, but—' She paused, looking over me and Ashu carefully. 'All of *this* is only for people who aren't fighting with each other. Anyone interested?'

Ashu spoke to me pretty quickly after that.

* * *

Ma came back later. A lot later than she said she would. But I told myself I wouldn't make a fuss otherwise she would start going away without telling me at all. The doorbell rang one-two-three-four-five times in a row, so quickly that Mrs Shome got annoyed and opened her mouth wide to shout at whoever it was, but when she saw it was Ma at the door, she stopped. Ma walked in clumsily and dropped her bag onto the floor like she had butterfingers. She also tripped over Ashu's shoes, and instead of scolding him for leaving them in the middle of the room, she laughed. She was in a good mood.

'Anita,' Ma said happily and asked to speak with her in the kitchen.

I waited for ten whole seconds before I tiptoed and stood near the kitchen door. Ashu followed me. The door was half-open, and we could see Mrs Shome pouring Ma a big glass of water. Ma drank it like she was very thirsty.

'Not sure this was such a good idea, Leela. The children—they're upset.'

Ma surprisingly still had black splotches on her face, but this time, I think it was because her make-up was all messy. 'It's fine, they'll be fine,' she said and poured herself more water. Some of it splashed onto the counter. 'Won't you ask me how it was?'

Mrs Shome gave a thin smile. 'I'm sure you'll tell me either way.'

Ma continued, 'He was great—different! Different, different, different.' It sounded like she was going to break into a song.

I glanced towards Ashu, but he wasn't looking back at me.

'Different from whom? The last guy? That—professor from the university?'

I raised my eyebrows at Ashu again to show that I didn't understand, but he kept listening attentively, his ear sticking to the door.

The two grown-ups were now muttering under their breath, and we missed some of the conversation.

'I swear. I won't anymore,' Ma said, her words running over each other.

'I'm driving you back.'

'Unnecessary, Anita.'

'Completely necessary.'

I agreed with Mrs Shome. When Ma is sleepy-and-tired, she drops things to the floor more easily. She also smells funny, like she has put a whole bottle of perfume onto herself and I want to say Ma! Stop. But I'm the child, and she's the Ma, so I can't. Ma shouldn't get sleepy when she drives us home because then she'll close her eyes and we'll crash into another car and die. I was so worried about that that I didn't smile even when Ashu shook my shoulders and said, 'It's fine, silly. I forgive you.' I gave a big sigh only when finally Mrs Shome took the keys from Ma's big handbag and drove us all home.

Later, Ma was lying down on the sofa in the room between mine and Ashu's, and hers. We call it a room, but really, it's quite small—small enough that I can leap across from one end to the other in two-and-a-half jumps and reach the dining table. I was sitting on the other end of the sofa.

Ashu was still writing something in his book at the table. I had never seen him care so much about homework.

'How was your dinner, Ma?' I asked.

'Interesting.' She lay her head back on the sofa. 'Come, press my head, sweetie.'

'Interesting like what?' I moved over to Ma's side and asked, reminding her of the game.

'Interesting—like jellybeans mixed with mustard and ketchup.'

I giggled. 'That sounds dis-gus-ting.'

'Don't knock it till you've tried it.'

I was pressing Ma's forehead like a piano, ding-ding-ding. My fingers went squishing into her skin, and I thought that maybe I could become a famous piano player someday. I started moving my fingers fast.

'Do it properly, Mira!' Ma snapped.

I slowed down. When I remembered what Ma had gone for, my stomach clenched again.

'Did—did Coach say anything about us?'

Ma laughed. 'He's a man of few words.'

Ashu looked up from his seat, saying the first thing to Ma in many hours. 'Are you seeing him again then?'

'Maybe.' Then after a pause, she said, 'But come to think of it, I'm cancelling your lessons.'

As though she were talking to herself, Ma nodded fast like a bobblehead toy. 'After yesterday—yep, I don't think the two of you should go swimming anymore.'

Ashu opened his mouth so wide that a giant bee could fly in. 'What about our life skills?' He made a funny wiggling action with two of his fingers, shifting in his seat.

'Plenty of other places you can learn those,' she said. 'And who taught you how to make air quotes?' She repeated the wiggling motion.

'Rahul,' Ashu said, sticking his chin up.

'Rahul, haan? That boy's too smart-alecky for his own good.'

'At least he's my friend.' Ashu was staring at his homework as he said this. His face was so still that it was almost like a ghost had spoken.

Ma said nothing. She got up to play some music on our radio. Suddenly the room was full of different sounds—trumpets and piano and drums—all at once and I wanted to say, Ma, stop, it's too loud! But Ma was enjoying the song. She was swaying like the trees in the wind, and a minute or two after, like she just noticed him, Ma stopped in front of Ashu.

'Come onnn, Ashu,' she said, flipping the pages of his holiday homework. 'Don't be so boring.'

Ashu kept his head down and he said nothing.

'Come, Ashu,' Ma said to him again, but this time she held out her hand and offered it to him. 'Let's quit our fight.'

I kept looking, wondering if Ashu would ignore Ma again and stay quiet. But he got up. I saw that his eyes were wet even though he still hung his head. He shuffled closer to Ma. 'I'm sorry,' he said to her in a soft voice.

Ma waved his sorry away. 'We were both idiots. Forget it.' She hugged him and gave him a quick, quick kiss, but only on his cheek, not on his ear. Then they pulled me into their hug too, so we were all one big hug-triangle, equal from all sides. No one loving each other more, and no one loving each other less.

Why is it that stars are born? Why do caterpillars turn into butterflies but not the other way around? How do planes fly and not sink? And pressure cookers? Why do they hiss like a snake but not teacups? Why does this woman only have one leg? And this man smush his face against the car window? Isn't it so funny, Ma? Ma? Isn't it funny? Why aren't you laughing? Can I go to the bathroom? Why don't we have a father? What were you like as a child? Will I grow taller next year? Do you love me more than you love Ashu? Who, what and why.

If someone—anyone—had warned me about the sheer number of inane questions that children asked, I would never have had them. Never popped them out of my belly—though it took hours and was more like a slow burn than a pop. Never have let that doctor with the handsome, crooked smile cut a knife through my stomach like it was his breakfast toast. Flap open the skin, let the kid out and zip me back up. Job done. Okay bye. Next. Well, in Ashu's time, it was the handsome doctor. In Mira's, there was a fussy old lady who, I bet, had never had a kid of her own and who stuck her face into my vagina and said, 'You've got to push harder, dear.' I would have pushed her nose back into her skull, had I the strength.

Most days, I deal with the questions with games that are just silly enough to be entertaining. The one where we describe days through food, for instance. That's my favourite. It gets me hungry. It distracts me. On foggy days, it drives the clouds away like a pigeon being chased off into the skies. I beat the kids at it left, right and centre. I wield answers, bend and twist words like a weapon—not a sharp-edged dagger but an arrow that you never saw coming in the first place.

But some days, even the games aren't enough. So I turn the questions into a challenge. I make up answers. I conjure up stories.

I tell them lies.

SURFACE

MIRA

Ma told me the story of my birth last week. We were in the kitchen making tomato and cucumber sandwiches for our tiffin. Ma had taken cold tomatoes out of the fridge and was spreading thick butter onto bread the same way she puts sunscreen on our skin. She was telling me that when she had me, she'd travelled to Finland which is not just full of fish but also people.

'Why Finland?' I asked.

'Do you want to hear the rest of the story or not?'

So Ma had me in springtime inside a lake next to many cottages, that's why it is called a waterbirth. We don't have much spring here where we live. We just have summer most of the time and only a few short days of feeling cold and Ma saying, 'Put on your socks' over and over again. Ashu and I used to sing 'You get shocks without socks' so we remembered, but Ma said it was annoying so we had to stop. 'Were you alone?' I said to Ma. Even though I had heard this story a few times before, I liked asking new questions about it whenever they went pop! in my head like bread in a toaster.

'Hmmm?' Ma said, sipping water from a glass.

'Was everybody with you? Your Ma? Pa? My Pa?'

Ma set the glass down and laughed roughly, sounding like she'd swallowed something disgusting like cough medicine. 'They didn't have the balls to stay in the room while I pushed you out.'

Although Ma says a lot of things I don't understand, I knew she wasn't talking about basketball.

'Room?' I nudged her.

'The lake,' Ma corrected herself. Ma often forgets her stories, but I am her little helper and make her remember.

'Were you happy to have me?' I loved this part.

'So happy. I felt happy like I was having a thousand jalebis on a cold day. I had always wanted a baby girl.'

'But what about Ashu?'

'Ashu isn't a girl.'

'Maaaaa. I know that.' I gave her the same look she always gives me after I make a bad joke.

'Ha-ha. I always wanted a girl, so I tried again after I had Ashu.'

'Tried what?'

'Oh, the questions.' Ma started wrapping the sandwiches in foil, and it made loud, crinkly sounds.

'What if I were a boy too?' I tried a different track. I perched myself up onto the counter so I could see Ma better.

Ma shook her head noisily, and her earrings spun around and made me dizzy, so I stopped looking at them. 'No. You couldn't be.'

'Why?'

'I just knew it.' Ma shut the tiffin boxes with a snap.

'How?'

'I knew it in my belly button that you were a girl.' Ma closed her eyes as if our talking was over.

'Ohhh.'

Ma feels things in her belly button that I can't feel even when I try really hard. She can tell what the weather will be the next day. She knows what time Ashu and I went to sleep (not the time we tell Ma in the morning but the real honest-to-God time). She can tell if I've really eaten my food at school or left it in some foil inside a desk. All she has to do is sit in peace for thirty minutes without me talking and touch her belly button. You need to be silent, she says, for it to work. And it's true! It works. Her belly button is never wrong.

Sometimes when Ma says these things—about boys and girls—I quickly look over to see if Ashu is listening. Does he feel sad that Ma wanted a girl more than a boy? I can't tell even though I am the world's greatest expert at knowing what Ashu is feeling. I know him the best. For example, when he licks the outside of his lip as if trying to reach leftover ice cream, it means that he is thinking hard and his brain is hurting. When he is confused or pretending to be, he raises one eyebrow up these days and stares at you. And when Ashu is sad, he looks like a mouse who just went swimming. His halfway voice becomes small, his eyes look wet and his nose starts to shake and quiver.

At school, once when I complained loudly in class about Ashu and his funny new voice, girls, who weren't even my friends, started talking to me. They told me all the horrible things their brothers did. Someone's younger brother burped in their face a million times in a row. Another girl's brother locked her in her room and didn't let her come out all day. Another girl's brother, who is a captain at our school, wrestled with her and twisted her arm until it hurt. They looked me expectantly when it was my turn to tell them what Ashu did.

I had to make up something quickly on the spot. 'He—he farts into bedcovers and doesn't laugh at my jokes,' I said.

They all looked at me like I was mad and walked away.

Ok, I thought later. I guess Ashu wasn't as bad as these girls' brothers. *They* sounded like monsters. But what they didn't realise is, even though Ashu doesn't do bad things, he's just plain annoying, especially when he doesn't want to hang out with me sometimes.

Most of the time, I can get my way around Ashu because I know that he loves me the most in the world, more than even Ma does. I can trouble him and he won't say anything. But once, Ashu came back from school in a really bad mood. He didn't smile at all no matter how many jokes or fun facts I told him. He didn't shout the way Ma does when she's angry. Instead, his face became red like a beetroot, like he was trying to hold all his screaming and shouting in. In the end, he looked at me and said under his breath, 'I don't want to talk to you right now, Mira. Make your own friends. Why don't you come back when you've grown up?' And he pulled the covers over himself.

He didn't call me a silly goose, he called me Mira. That's when I knew that something was really wrong. Besides, didn't Ashu know? Maybe Rahul was his best friend, but Ashu was mine. I haven't really got friends at school because the other girls say that I'm weird and that I make up stories.

But it was all okay because I had a plan. I went to the bathroom and locked it for an hour even though Ashu came and banged the door and said he really needed to pee. I sat on the toilet seat and touched my belly button with my index finger to know when

1. I would grow up
2. Get my own friends
3. Both of the above

I sat there quietly, even though my finger and my arm ached and I was bored. I only got out of the bathroom when Ma yelled Mira! Get out, you've been holed up in there for too long! But nothing had changed. Ma was still in her room, reading her book. Ashu was back to throwing a basketball at the wall and catching it when it bounced.

And the only thing I had managed to do with my belly button was remove some dirt.

ASHU

Ashu sat on the stairs waiting. It had been nearly an hour since he had been there, on the steps outside Rahul's flat. He had watched multiple flip-flopped, dirty-soled feet brush past him. He had followed a family of ants that crawled over his legs and onto the parched white wall till they disappeared inside it. He had stared at the sun.

A couple of times, a maid had shouted at him for being in the way and he had moved to the top of the staircase and then back. Normally, Ashu didn't mind being made to wait. He was endlessly patient with Mira no matter how much time she took to finish a story, and she often did take the long way around to make her point. It didn't trouble him that Ma made him wait in the car for her when she went to the shops and didn't return for ages. Or that sometimes she had Mira and him hang around the whole day to go with her somewhere, and it turned out later that she simply forgot to take them anywhere at all.

But it was past three now, a whole hour after Rahul said he would be home, and Ashu was starting to feel restless. He hadn't met Rahul since the day at the pool. Ashu had been embarrassed by the turn of events and hadn't called him after that. But now, Rahul was leaving for his Nani's. Every summer, he was gone for two, sometimes three weeks, during which they spoke on the phone sometimes, Ashu twisting the coil of his landline and Rahul replying haltingly through the commotion at his end. These calls were unsatisfying and scratchy, like spreading cold butter on toast, but at least they were something.

Ashu wanted to say goodbye, spend a few good hours doing something fun before Rahul left and summer stretched out in front of him. But that wasn't all, Ashu suspected, as he shook his legs impatiently. He was also—for the first time—perhaps nervous about meeting his friend. Maybe it was the feeling of pinpricks behind his knees if they knocked over Rahul's and stayed there when they were sitting next to each other. Or the feeling he had if they nestled too close in the car. Sometimes, it was the need to call him, tell him everything that had happened in the day, even if they had just spent several hours together at school. And it was the desire to, somehow, even though Ashu was smaller and shorter and, in general, much less brave than Rahul was, protect him from everything he knew.

Ashu shook his head and tried to think about something else, when to his relief there was the sound of a car, the biting of gravel, the rising of dust to free him from his thoughts. He got up quickly and walked towards the small white car that had just rolled in. He was finding it difficult to keep his legs steady although he had had no trouble getting to Rahul's place earlier that day. His hands felt strangely cold too.

'Hi,' Rahul's eyes crinkled in the sun as he exited the car.

'Hey.'

As Rahul raised his arms to lift a few bags from the car, Ashu saw that Rahul had grown even taller than him these last few months, a fact that he seemed to notice only now after a brief absence. Ashu had to crane his neck to see him. There, in the shadows, he observed pale lines that had formed on the back of his friend's waist, merging with his tanned skin. Ashu had seen marks like these on Ma before, but whenever he pointed them out, she covered herself loosely with a shawl and muttered, looking at Mira and him, 'No thanks to you two.' If he were honest, on Ma, he found those stretch marks ugly, like scars—but here, finding them unexpectedly on Rahul's skin, they looked majestic, like the stripes of a tiger.

Ashu had been so occupied with his thoughts that he barely realised when Rahul's parents got out of the car and went up the stairs. At least his mother had squeezed Ashu's shoulder to say hello. His father had just walked past them.

'What's behind your back?' Rahul asked.

Ashu had brought along a packet of green Uncle Chipps that were only available in the store near his house. He tossed it at Rahul. 'Since you're going to a village,' Ashu said, 'I thought you might end up needing some real food.'

But Ashu had forgotten that in his wait, he had got a bit hungry and had helped himself to the chips. As the plastic went fluttering through the air, a few stray pieces fell dramatically to the ground.

Rahul laughed, catching the bag, and dug into the half-empty packet. 'Rampur,' he said in a muffled voice, 'is not a village. You know, they're planning to open a McDonald's in the next ten years. I heard whispers.'

'Ten years?' Ashu mock-widened his eyes. 'Wow, that's impressive. And what's the running water situation again?'

'Er,' Rahul caught his eye. 'They're working on it.'

Ashu and Rahul were almost always in a hurry when they met because someone would tell them off for making too much noise, or Ma would wonder where Ashu was, or they'd both have to rush home to finish their homework. Right now, too, Ashu and Rahul only had half an hour before Rahul had to run upstairs. He had to catch his train tonight, and then he'd be gone. Though it was only a few weeks, Ashu could already tell that it was going to feel much longer. That no matter how much Ashu practised football by himself, or made up games with Mira, or watched episodes and episodes of bad TV, the hours would dangle in front of him threateningly and the days would stretch. And Ashu would wait for this time to come to a slow end, like watching the last drops of water fall from a closed tap.

MIRA

There are three people in our family, but once, there were four. I used to think that it had always been just Ma and Ashu and me. But at school during a project, I found out that most people in class had four, five, sometimes even ten people in their families. Everyone in class looked at me with wide eyes when I said I had never had a father, not even for a little bit, not at all. When some of the older kids in school found out too, they called Ma lots of bad words I didn't know the meaning of—like divorced and slut and whore which sounds like wild boar—and they started to laugh. So I began to ask Ma questions.

Sometimes Ma said she picked me and Ashu up from the shops when she was in the mood, but they didn't have a return policy, so she had to keep us. But mostly, when I asked about our father, Ma didn't say anything at all. She just looked away, and no matter how much I poked her or pulled her hair or even danced around her to make her laugh, she kept quiet.

I found a photograph under Ma's mattress one day when I was looking for sweets in her room. The photo had two people: Ma—and I think, our father. They were next to a fountain in the photo. Ma was smiling. She was wearing jeans and sitting on the ground and our father was lying next to her. He had the funniest coloured pants on—red—and short black hair with one curl that went up flick! into the sky. I grabbed the photo and ran out of Ma's room. When Ashu saw it, he had tears in his eyes because he realised that even though he was older than me, I was a much better detective than he was. We both agreed to put the photograph back in Ma's room the next day before she could find out. But for that one night only, we stayed up, looking at it and making up stories.

'Ashu,' I asked him carefully after I realised something. 'Where are *we*?'

'Oh—I don't know,' he squinted at the photo. 'This must have been taken in Delhi—before we were born.'

I didn't want to make it obvious, but I was pretty surprised. I just nodded and said Of Course, which is the grown-up version of Ok and shows that you understand. But the truth is, I'd never thought about Ma without us or even before us. I thought she'd always just been our Ma—the same way I used to once think that she didn't have her own name. She does, and she hates it.

Sometimes, Ma gets a phone call that she calls a 'courtesy call' after hanging up. When she is on such a call, Ma either stays silent or makes faces or says no-no-no—nothing else. I like to guess who Ma might be talking to and what she might be talking to them about. I try to find out from Ma's voice whether she is happy or sad. If it's someone nice like Mrs Shome or someone scary who makes Ma's voice become tiny like a mouse's, or someone from Ma's-family-before-us.

Ma got one such 'courtesy call' the first few days of summer holidays, but after talking, she didn't even say bye, she just hung up the phone with a big wham! and walked out of the room.

Ashu didn't know who it was either. What's the point of Ashu being five years older than me, I wonder sometimes, if he never tells me anything useful? He didn't warn me, for instance, that the sports teacher at school, who taught Ashu too, scolded you if you chewed gum in front of him. He didn't tell me that people in class didn't like it if you had short hair and talked a lot. He never remembers anything real about our father either. He only says something vague—like our father used to hold Ashu up high in the air to get sweets from the khoi bag at birthday parties. Or that he had hands that were sticky like mithai syrup. Now, what am I supposed to do with that?

But, really, if you ask me, Ma isn't any better. When aunties at parties or parent-teacher meetings ask her about her family, she says, 'Have none,' even though Ashu and I are standing right there next to her. When they ask her if she has a husband, Ma cocks her head to one side and makes a clicking sound with her teeth. And when they look shocked and their eyes pop out, she smiles and tells us later in the car that that's what you get for being interfering.

But worst of all, Ma forgets so much that if anyone asks about her siblings and Ma is in the mood to reply, she says, 'I'm an only child. Thank god, right?' and Ashu and I raise our eyebrows so high at each other that they fully disappear under our hair.

That summer—the summer in which I first began smoking cigarettes—was spent outside a pharmacy in Delhi. It was a small one that stood squished between a tea stall and a parking lot, and everyone—the girls from college, aunties from the neighbourhood, men in crushed white shirts on their break from work, rich kids who wore baggy clothes and pretended to be poor, and poor kids who tried to look rich—they all spent time there. Hiding, waiting, drinking hot tea, smoking. I used to find it so ironic at seventeen, standing in front of posters of 'no smoking' and charred lungs, all plastered on dirty glass walls, puffing out rings.

After the deed, I'd go back home from college and sit on my bed and watch television in the drawing room outside from the corner of my eye. My father, who was slim despite years of sitting on the sofa, would usually have put on the seventh Harrison Ford film of the week. The house felt like a boombox, with dialogue and movie gunshots constantly bouncing from one wall to the other. Through the thin wall in my room came the loud, rough voice of my elder sister who was forever talking to someone on the phone. While her propensity to talk endlessly annoyed me, I admired her for it all the same. It took a certain level of arrogance to assume the world wanted to listen to you.

From outside came another series of sounds—the clattering of pots and pans, a ringing of bells, the lighting of camphor, the chanting of prayers to god. My mother stood in the puja room, praying night and day for the health of my father, the health of the neighbours, the health of the world. She forgot, as she twisted the rosary beads and murmured chants underbreath, to include herself in those prayers. She feared god more than she loved him. I found her often staring at the wall, waiting for a figure to transgress the plaster. In the thin plastic notebooks that sat in her bedside drawer, scrawled with notes and chants, were things she wanted to ask him if she ever came across him. At times she prayed for me. Apparently, I had been an obstinate child who, after a series of events, had to be sent to a convent school to be straightened out.

And now suddenly, at seventeen, I was free. After years of being cloistered with girls my age, mean and striking, here I was, in college, plunged into a space with boys.

It alarmed me how much they had grown in the years I had not been around them. Suddenly, the boys were taller, their shoulders broader. Their voices had deepened like valleys. We tried to coexist together, the girls and boys. Hormones tumbled on top of each other. I was amused by how easy it was to make them listen, how little it seemed to take. I went on a few dates, most of them cheap, unremarkable, but at least they gave me something to do.

I took English as my core subject. I liked reading and listening to the words roll over me in class when the teacher with the hoarse voice read a passage out loud. Often, I hid a different novel under my desk, reading something of my own.

The other girls in class were not half bad. I made two friends, Maithali and Khushbu, whose homes I went to sometimes after college. During the day, after skipping class, we drank cheap vodka at a shady bar whose only occupants were teenagers and unemployed men. The men looked at us in the dim bar, and we laughed and had shots. In the harsh light of day, on our way back to campus, we threw up during the auto ride. At night, we sat and listened to music and smoked joints and secretly wondered why we all hung out together. They were smart, the girls, but not good-looking. That's why I was the most surprised when Maithali announced that she was going steady with the boy popular for having disrupted the principal's inaugural speech that year with a rock performance.

'Nikhil?' I asked her.

She nodded happily and held a pile of folders to her stomach. 'Isn't he amazing?'

'Yeah,' I said, before sipping my hot coffee. 'He's cute.'

MIRA

Ma takes out the globe and spins it one-two-three. She does this every year when it's so hot outside that the bright orange flowers on the gulmohar tree in our lane get burnt and crispy and we are home from school on vacation. We climb on top of the tall chair and reach into the cupboard where Ma keeps the things we don't use much. Then we catch the globe before it falls onto the floor. The cupboard has lots of things like our old clothes and schoolbooks, presents we got that Ma wants to gift to other people even though we want to keep them, and the globe. Ashu got the globe as a birthday present from Mrs Shome when he turned twelve two years ago. But after he and I almost broke it playing catch, Ma stuffed it into the cupboard of useless things for 'safekeeping.'

Usually, after Ma dusts off the globe, and we go cough-cough, we sit down around it and start the game. Here are the rules. When Ma says three, we have to place our finger on the globe and stop it from getting dizzy. This way we can decide where we are going for a holiday. Ma always says, 'Anywhere in the world you want.' But really, I'll be honest, Ma is very picky.

One year, when Ashu's finger landed on Paris which is in France with the Eiffel Tower, Ma put a fancy hat on her head and spoke in a high voice with a funny accent: 'Ooh la la, but eet eez too hot dere, dese time of year. Pick anozer place, monsieur.'

Ashu laughed and was going to try again until I reminded him that it was not monsieur's turn but mine. Another time, my finger landed on Brazil in South America, and instantly Ashu giggled though there was nothing funny about it at all. Ashu laughs at absolutely nothing sometimes. Ma shushed him and told him not to be juvenile. Brazil was obviously too far.

Today, Ma's finger stopped on Antarctica where the penguins live. I have a big fat book about penguins and looked them up. Turns out penguins don't have any teeth—wisdom or milk or any. They simply swallow their food whole without chewing it and it goes straight plonk! into their stomach. It would be pretty cool to meet penguins and see how they do that, but we can't go there now because it's very cold and also it is very lonely.

Maybe one day when we spin the globe we'll find the perfect place for us to visit. Not too hot, not too cold, not too far and not super close either. But because we can't decide now, we are going to the same place we always do which is close to home. It's a lot of fun, and Ma is very happy whenever we go there, and no one fights with anyone. Unfortunately, this time, we are not going alone.

FLOAT

MIRA

'Do you know who I am?'

I stared up at her face and stretched my neck nice and long so I could see her better even though the sun was coming into my eyes. I took a good look and decided that Ma's sister looks nothing like Ma.

She has:

1. One large and oily-like-samosa forehead
2. Two gold cavity fillings in her front teeth
3. No mole on her cheek or face or anywhere

She didn't say anything to my 'hello.' Instead, she pulled me into a hug and asked me this question. Did she forget who she was and want someone to remind her? I almost asked her this, but before I could, she laughed and said, 'Of course you don't! What am I saying? Last time I met you, you were this small.' She hovered her right hand near her knees.

We were all outside the airport entrance. For the past half an hour, Ashu and I had been balancing our bums on the metal railing for people who wait. We kept swinging our legs front-and-back back-and-front and counting the number of airplanes in the sky.

I counted five, but Ashu insisted there had been only four. There were many people around us, including confused men standing with chart papers that said funny things like WELCOMME MR GOOGLY SAMSON and NAMASTEY, MS. JODDIE BUTTRESS. Some were holding other things, too, like big bouquets of flowers and boxes of chocolate. But we didn't carry anything at all. We waited for a long time, and finally they came out with their suitcases.

When Ma told us that she had a sister, but she hadn't met her for a few years, I didn't believe her. When I don't see Ashu for an hour, even two, I feel strange in my tummy, the same way I do when I say a small lie to Ma. If Ashu's just in the other room pretend-doing homework but really just daydreaming, I keep going over to him and pulling silly faces until he gets mad and says Mira! I'm going to tickle you! and I have to run away. And if he's gone out, like to play with Rahul or something, I keep looking at the clock and wondering when he'll be back to play with me.

Ma's sister now came towards Ashu and draped her arms around him. But Ashu just stood there awkwardly. His own long arms were by the side of his body, flopping around like spider-legs from left to right. Ashu is good at hugs. He is just not good at hugging strangers.

Last in line for a hug was Ma, who looked like she was playing (and winning) Statue. Her eyes and nose and lips were hardly moving, even when Ma's sister touched her arm and said, 'Long time, Leela.'

I could tell that Ma didn't like her sister the same way she didn't like:

1. Me and Ashu when we ask too many questions
2. Waiters that are very slow
3. Male shower-nest pigs
4. People in the admin department except for Mrs Shome

I glanced at Ashu, and he raised his eyebrows at me. Actually, he only raised one, which is his newest trick. He goes around the house raising one eyebrow at everything—the lights when the electricity goes off, the bed when it's soaking with rain, even his homework when he is bored of doing it. I practised doing the one-eyebrow raise in the mirror, but when I couldn't, I used my finger to lift my eyebrow. I did that right now too.

Ashu and I both knew what Ma was thinking. She hated it when people said things like 'long time.' She told me once that it was what people said to fill silences.

'What's wrong with that?' I asked. 'Filling silences?'

'It means that you have an insipid, vacuous mind and aren't comfortable in your skin.'

I thought about all the times I sang or troubled Ashu or said a joke when there was silence. Although I had no idea what an insipidvacuous mind was, I was sure it wasn't a good thing.

Ma's sister pushed a young girl towards us. So far, she had been standing behind her, with a pair of earphones on her head. 'Avni, don't be rude,' Ma's sister said loudly. 'Meet your cousins.'

Avni slowly yanked her headphones down to her neck and walked towards me and Ashu. Honestly, she didn't really look like she wanted to be there.

'Hey,' she said.

I tried to copy her. 'Heyyy.'

She stared at Ashu, but he was in a Mood, maybe because Ma made him wear pants instead of shorts or maybe because he had bad dreams. 'Hi,' he mumbled and tried to look away.

In the corner, the grown-ups were talking. But the three of us were quiet. I tried to make us talk too. 'What's your age?' I asked Avni.

'Fifteen,' she shrugged. 'My dad says I look older though. And so does my boyfriend.' Before I could ask her anything, she spoke to Ashu again. 'What about you?'

'I'm fifteen too.'

'What?' I swivelled towards him. 'Shadap, you're fourteen.'

His face turned red like a pomegranate. 'I turn fifteen in eleven months,' he said now.

'Whatever,' said Avni. 'You look tall enough to be my age.'

Ashu smiled. I looked at him properly—he wasn't *that* tall. Just a little bit more than me. Before I could say that to Avni, Ma and her sister pushed us inside the car.

'Come on, let's all catch up over food,' Ma's sister said, putting her arm around Ma now. 'Really, Leela. You just disappeared. It's been a long, long time.'

We went to a big fancy restaurant near the airport where the waiters look at you in the eye—and not just at your Ma—and say, 'What would you like to have, ma'am?' Most people call me by my name. Ashu calls me silly. People at school sometimes say that I am a nerd. One time, someone from the pizza company even called me 'sir' on the phone and Ashu made so much fun of me after that that I never called them back. So when the waiter called me ma'am, I puffed up my chest with pride and picked up the menu and went tap-tap-tap at all the things I liked, even though Ma made me change it later.

During lunch, I kept looking at Avni. Her hair was short and only flicked the top of her shoulder. She ate everything slowly like she wasn't hungry. We had ordered pizza, and the grown-ups had ordered something called a risotto which looked like rice and milk. Pretty disgusting. I learnt only recently that when you add the word pretty in front of another word it means 'a little.' For example, I can say that Ashu is pretty lame. Or Ma is pretty pretty. Or Avni is pretty bored. And Aunty is pretty loud.

Ma's sister turned to us and said, 'What's this aunty-aunty

business? Call me Mausi. We are not Americans.' She then spoke to Ma, who was concentrating on the plate in front of her. 'Leela, do the kids not speak in Hindi? I've heard them go chattar-pattar in every other language, including one I don't understand.'

I grinned at Ashu. We had learnt P-language when we didn't want grown-ups around us to know what we were talking about.

Mausi sighed. 'Well, I suppose, at least they talk. This Avni keeps walking around with headphones and singing English songs. At least *we* had some culture growing up. Hai na?'

'Well,' said Ma, speaking for the first time in a while. 'We had a lot of other shit too.'

Mausi kept talking like Ma hadn't said a bad word. 'I can't even get Avni to join any extra-curriculars.'

Ma, to my surprise, replied. 'Ashu doesn't believe in reading books either. And this one,' she tugged at me, 'had a troubled experience swimming recently, so now even that's done.'

Ashu, Avni and I looked at each other. I had no idea how somehow the whole conversation had become about us. We had just been sitting quietly and eating. I could tell we all wanted to groan.

After we finished our food, Ma asked Mausi, 'So, when will you be back?'

'The conference is meant to be a week-long one, but you know how these things go.'

'I wouldn't know. I just work at an office job, remember?' Ma said pretty sharply.

'I didn't mean it like that.' Mausi winced. 'I mean—I'll be back to pick her up before the end of the month.'

Ma nodded. 'Right. And where's—?'

'Raman's travelling abroad too—important fair to attend. Thanks, really, for bailing us out. I wouldn't have asked, but there was no option.'

'It's fine,' Ma said, taking a sip of water. Then she added, 'Don't worry about it.'

When the bill came, Ma and Mausi wrestled over it like they were playing tug-of-war. At the end, Mausi won and stuffed some notes under the bill like it was a big secret.

'You shouldn't have. You're the one visiting,' Ma said half-heartedly. I noticed she hadn't tried to pull the tray towards herself as much as Mausi did.

'Leela, please. It's the least I can do.' She bared her big-cavity teeth and squeezed Ma's arm. Ma didn't smile back.

* * *

In the holiday car, which is just our yellow car but on vacation, I can stretch my legs out and make them play like drum sticks on the seat in front. I can wiggle my fingers, from the back of Ashu's head to the front, and say Surprise! to scare him. Ashu and I can eat crumbly snacks like Lay's Magic Masala chips and aloo bhujiya that fall all over the car, even if it's the wrong time of the day and even if it's right before a meal. We can dance, hop, roll down windows and stick our noses out to say hello to every person, tree and stray dog on the road. Sometimes Ma plays games with us—but never the boring game of what shape a cloud is. Sometimes she tells us to shut up and sleep.

Because we had never had anybody else with us on our trip before, Ma said we had to be polite and ask the guest where she wanted to sit, that's the rule. So, this time, like every time, I didn't get to sit in the front, but good news, Ashu couldn't either. Instead, he had to climb into the back with me, and Avni hopped into the front.

When Avni first came to stay with us, I was really excited to have a sister. Avni is beautiful. Her hair shines and is dark black like the sweet jamun that sometimes falls off the trees near the park. And it's so short that when she puts her hair in a ponytail, it hardly fits and sticks out like the eraser at the end of a pencil.

Ma told us to clean the house before Mausi dropped her off, so that Avni would be comfortable. We kept a gadda on the floor in our room because there was no space anywhere else. There was Ma's bed, but Ma's bed is always Ma's, and she only lets us sleep there with her if we are feeling really sick or have very scary dreams. So, we went around dusting and cleaning the house. Ma took out a big patterned bedsheet and went flap-flap-flap three times until it fell neatly over the gadda for Avni. Then I fluffed up the pillow making it soft and squishy and kept a teddy bear that I used when I was much smaller in case Avni needed it.

But when we entered the house, Avni wrinkled her nose as though she could smell something bad and asked where her room was. When Ma told her that she had to share a room with Ashu and me and had a gadda to herself, she went quiet like she didn't feel like talking. In fact, she didn't want to speak to me much at all. She spoke to Ashu a lot more than she spoke to me, which wasn't fair because he already has his own friend.

'What? Rahul has gone to his Nani's,' Ashu shrugged. 'Don't be a baby.'

I followed Avni around for the first two days, but she was always listening to her headphones or with Ashu. I tried to tickle her on her foot, and she told me not to touch her without her permission. I knotted a handkerchief and held it underneath her nose when she was sleeping to make her sneeze, but she turned around and kicked me away. I asked to borrow her headphones in my politest tone, the one I use with strangers, but she told me that I had greasy ears and would ruin them.

But now, Ma told Avni to remove her headphones because we were travelling as a family and were all going to listen to songs together. This made Avni huff and puff a little like the wolf from that story except we are not little pigs, especially not Ma. Ma was in a great mood. She had rolled down the windows and was singing along with us. And even though she usually said that we looked like dogs when we stuck our faces out, with our tongues wagging, she didn't say anything right now. She even made the music louder for us and drove the car faster, so we all felt like we were actors from a movie.

'Can someone please tell me where we're going?' Avni asked for the millionth time.

'You'll seeeeee.' I was jumping in my seat. Ma, Ashu and I had decided to keep it a surprise for Avni because we were going to the best place in the world—better than even Paris and Brazil and Antarctica. We were going to the farm, where Ma takes us every year. They grow mangoes there, big juicy ones that hang from trees just like I do on the jungle gym. But instead of normal yellow mangoes, these ones are green and are cut into thin long slices with salt and chilli powder on them. At the farm, the air is hot in the day and at night, sometimes, we can see fireflies sparkling like stars.

At the farm, time is also stretchy like a rubber band. It is the only period in the whole year when we have Ma with us from morning to evening to night. No Mrs Shome, no office, no anyone at all. Ma sits on the hammocks that hang from the mango trees and reads for hours. She doesn't mind if Ashu and I spend afternoons in the sun and get tanned. She doesn't even care that we run around and get dirty from all the dust and mud.

So I knew that there was no way Avni would not love the place. And if she loved it, she would love us, and then she would want me as a sister forever.

After we had been driving for a while, we saw the big yellow-and-red sign on the side of the road and stopped the car. Ma said we all had to go to the bathroom to wash our hands. The three of us girls went in one direction, but Ashu had to go to the other side for boys. Ma, Avni and I sat in stalls next to each other. I was the fastest, then Avni and then Ma. I couldn't hear what Ma was doing in the washroom, and I yelled out to her from my stall. But she shushed me and told me it was rude to ask. Afterwards, we pumped a pink liquid from a bottle which had more water than soap, and swished our hands together. Ma draped paper napkins around my hands and went round and round till I almost looked like a mummy myself—only an Egyptian one—and we all laughed. Later, Avni tiptoed towards Ma and said something in her ear, and Ma smiled back like they were on the same team. I bit my lip.

Usually, Ma doesn't like us eating from McDonald's. She says that the food is greasy and gives people gas. Ashu and I like to imagine a cloud of gas coming out of people's bums, like a train. Choo-choo! But Ma doesn't mind these things on our holiday.

The sofa-seat we were on was bright red and felt like Play-Doh. I was squishing my fingers in it when Avni reminded me that I'd just washed my hands.

'What were you whispering to Ma in the bathroom?' I asked her.

Ashu and Ma, who had gone to order the food, sat down with two big trays. I grabbed two of the French fries and popped them in my mouth.

Avni glanced at Ma and Ashu, then said, 'I—I had got my period, so—'

'What's a period?'

Ma exchanged a look with Avni. Then she took a deep sigh and said, 'It's something painful that happens to your body. It'll happen to you in a few years too.'

We began eating our food. I stuffed some more French fries into my mouth before I asked 'Wait, what about Ashu?'

'Won't happen to him,' said Ma.

'Why not?'

'Just one of life's cruel mysteries.'

I felt Avni shake with laughter, and I suddenly felt irritated. I tried to act as if I couldn't hear her at all. I noticed that Ashu was doing that too.

'But what does it look like? This period thing?'

'Like—' Ma looked around the table. She grabbed a long ketchup bottle and squeezed a big swipe of red onto her burger, '—this.'

All three of us, Avni, Ashu and I shuddered, even though Avni was laughing a second earlier.

'Like movie blood?' I dropped my voice down to a whisper.

'Real blood,' said Ma, biting into her burger, the swipe of red now disappearing inside her mouth.

'Every month.' She dabbed her mouth clean with the back of her hand.

'Ma—' Ashu said gingerly. He looked funny in the face. 'Can we talk about something else right now?'

'Why? Are you feeling queasy? You're the one likely to make a girl pregnant. You need to know this better than Mira.'

I didn't know what a period had to do with making girls pregnant. But I did know that it was Ashu who looked red now. We ate the rest of our food in silence.

Towards the end, Ma stepped out for five minutes for fresh air, but when she came back, she didn't smell fresh. Instead, she smelt strange and dirty, like a bonfire. Before I could ask her anything about it, she said, 'Hurry up, Mira. Questions later. Don't you want to get going?'

When we got back into the car, every one of us, even Avni, opened the windows and sang along with the woman on the radio, so the whole world could hear us loud and clear. In the backseat, Ashu and I sat cross-legged, looked outside and saw the roads becoming narrower and bumpier and the world becoming greener, and we yelled loudly from the bottom of our throats. And even though I didn't have a best friend like Rahul, and Avni still didn't like me, and Ma said that one day I'd get something painful called a period, I stuck my head out of the window and laughed.

My parents made no claims to being modern. In my second year of college, they began to matchmake for my sister. She was four years older than me, had graduated from college nearly eighteen months ago and still had no job nor any romantic prospects. So, the search began.

A steady stream of families entered my house those days. Boys solicited by my parents to come look at my sister, to ascertain if they were destined to marry in just the span of an hour. Boys masquerading as men. I began to use classes as an excuse to slip out of my own domestic drama, but often I came back home from college and found more pairs of shoes by our doorway than before. That would be the first clue. My mother, the second. She'd glare at me, hurt but not surprised that I had forgotten a family was coming to see my sister. I'd watch from the corner, entertained by the charade.

I thought that my sister would find the proceedings funny as well, but she'd shrug apathetically when I'd ask her about it, as if to say, it was bound to happen sooner or later.

One day, a family of three knocked on our door. A mother, shrunk and stiff like ours; a father, thin, tall but present. My sister and her prospective husband were seated across each other and both sets of parents mirrored each other's gestures. One tucked a loose strand of hair into a bun, the other followed; one clenched his forearm a little too tightly, the other clenched his even harder. They seemed to say: We're tired. We're tired of looking for love for our children. This is even harder than looking for it for ourselves. Let's stop. Let's make this work.

When the phone call came late that night, my parents were ecstatic. It's fixed, they clapped their hands together and exclaimed and began calling up their relatives, already planning the boxes of mithai, counting their silver coins. I slunk back into my room amidst the celebrations.

My sister's fiancé visited home quite a lot those days. I found them together often, whispering to each other like they hadn't met just a couple of weeks ago. He would mumble something to her and she'd giggle. When they thought I wasn't looking, they held hands. I was trying to cram for my exams one evening but couldn't focus with all the noise coming from the living room. I stormed outside to yell at my sister but saw her with her fiancé. He was holding a magnifying glass to her ears, and she was laughing endlessly, like it was the funniest thing she had ever seen in the world. I looked away.

I don't think there was ever really a time that my sister and I were close, although we had shared the same bed growing up. I always seemed to rub my sister off the wrong way. I used to shirk my duties, letting my share fall on her—things like answering the door in the afternoons when our mother took a nap or setting the table. Our mother liked us to place mats in precise patterns like her life depended on it.

Even when I was just a child, I remember my sister looked personally offended. She always watched me with a hint of anger, as though I had had a role in the decision to be born. She hid my toys, smacked me on my face when our mother wasn't looking, but denied this completely as we got older.

Sometimes, I wonder if she agreed to the wedding because she no longer wanted to stay with me. As though there were an unsaid rule that only one of the two of us could occupy the same space at the same time. That one would trample over the other. Or that both of us would take too much energy in one area and simultaneously combust.

In the days leading up to the wedding, my mother began devoting more of her time and attention towards my sister, who could never put a finger out of place. It was my sister she brought close to her knee and cradled like an overgrown baby when she had a headache. If my sister came home, bursting into tears from an event in the day, my mother would loosen her sari and extended the cloth that hung unattached towards her face to wipe her tears gently.

I didn't cry much. I found it strange, the way that people expressed every emotion they felt. I preferred to keep my feelings inside, safe, tucked in where they belonged, not spilling out like spit and blood. One day, I was shutting a drawer when my mother entered my room. I pushed the drawer so quickly that I didn't realise my finger had got stuck inside its rough edge. It was a small hurt, a little faint line that formed on my skin where blood had begun to pool. I had been hurt like that several times when I was younger and seemed to leave parts of my body where they didn't belong—my thumb in a cupboard, my big toe at the intersection of the door hinge. Right then, I began to cry. My mother, who had never seen me cry so much before, looked on in horror. I was wailing like a child who could neither be reasoned with nor controlled. She came closer and made me sit down on the bed. There it was, that patterned end of the sari that she usually offered to my sister. I tilted my neck so she could comfort me, wipe the hurt off, take it away. But she held my jaw firmly and scrubbed my skin where the tears had been like it was a dirty dish. Then she released my face and went back to her task. At the end of it, it was the same old story that I had always been vaguely aware of: my sister was worthy of love; I was not.

* * *

Just when I thought we were done with visitors for a while, I found, one day, a new row of worn shoes outside our door. My parents hastened me in when I entered the living room. I walked clenching my shoulders, not knowing what to expect. There was a man, not unattractive, sitting between two adults. He shuffled his feet often, but his gaze was gently fixed on me. It was quiet and disconcerting, and I tried to catch my parents' eyes to avoid his. But my mother stared steadfastly at the tray of tea and snacks she had prepared, and my father talked about the news. The meeting was short, I was uncommunicative. It ended before we knew it. Later, after the door clicked shut, I shouted at my parents. How they could bring a marriage proposal for me? Hadn't they just made arrangements to get rid of one daughter? Besides, I was so young. I wasn't even done with college.

My mother ventured forth gingerly: The boy had lost his parents when he was younger. His uncle and aunt—they were such nice people, she stressed. The boy was earning well too. And they called a second time. 'He really likes you.'

I didn't talk to them for a week until they slowly stopped pestering me about it.

* * *

My sister eventually got married and left. We were siblings born from the same river, and this was the first time the waters had parted. In the years to come, our lives would flow farther and farther away from each other. But we didn't know that then.

Maybe it was the negative space in the house where my sister once used to sit, where she used to eat, but my mother started to notice me more. She began to pray solely for me, focusing her energies on the one daughter who was wild and unruly. I made a fuss when she gathered vapours from the evening agarbatti and waved them to me with cupped hands; I frowned if she put a large red dot on my forehead after a puja. But secretly, I was pleased.

I was at home the week my mother went on a trip to the hills. She had been planning a visit to a temple in the foothills of the Himalayas for years. Most of the religious men and women that she knew, even her brother whom she was barely speaking to by this point, had already visited the site. But she'd always had my sister and me to look after, her hands were full, what could she do?

However, now that my sister had got married and left, all this time in my mother's day freed up. After taking permission from my father, my mother packed a bag and went.

My father and I began to spend a little time together. Prior to this, we never really had a need to communicate. It wasn't unusual for weeks to pass without a meaningful word exchanged between us. It was fine, we were both comfortable that way. We watched the occasional TV show together, but with my sister and mother between us. However, now things were different.

That Sunday evening, we were watching a comedy film. We were at the point of a ridiculous phone conversation between a man's lover and his ex-wife. The two of them had no idea who the other was, and both were incredibly sure that the other had dialled a wrong number. Then, suddenly, the man appeared on screen and began kissing the lover while she held the phone. It was unexpectedly scandalous, and both my father and I lunged at the TV remote to change the channel. We accidentally hit each other in the process and laughed like never before.

He then changed the channel to one airing a more suitable show about a pious woman. 'Looks like your mother, doesn't she?' I grinned because it was true.

My father placed his hand over his mouth, maybe realizing he had done a disservice to his wife by making fun of her in front of me. I wanted to tell him that it was okay.

The phone rang.

'Must be her.' He looked at the clock. My mother usually called us around 1 p.m. when she had access to the landline at her hotel.

I picked up the phone.

'Hello—'

'Tell her we are spending time together,' my father called out.

I pressed the receiver close to my ear to be able to listen to her through all the static.

'Why didn't you pass the phone to me?' he said, lowering the volume of the television, when I came back to sit on the sofa.

I said nothing, for my mother was dead.

The last time I saw my mother, she was lying still under a rough cotton sheet on the floor. We must have had an hour with her to ourselves, then people began to intrude. They swarmed into our home, filled up the space with their sweat and sympathy. They looked deeply into our eyes, waiting for a teardrop to fall so they could be the ones to wipe it away.

I cleared up stained cups of chai that people drank and left behind on the counter. I didn't set placemats on the table for the food made without onion and garlic. I was asked by an aunt I couldn't recognise to light an incense stick near my mother's body. I followed the instruction mindlessly, lighting the tip of the agarbatti each time the tall sticks crumbled to ash. It was only later that I realised that the agarbatti was meant to mask the smell of my mother's decaying body, as though she were a stale orange left in the sun for too long. When they took her away that evening, there were just flecks of ash left on the floor. I sat there and looked at the ash for hours, until the sun collapsed and the roof folded over and nothing was the same, yet everything was.

In the depths of the nights after, in the shallows of the mornings, I could hear my father's heels slapping against the cement floor, his fingers drumming against the head of his bed. I stayed home for a few days, but the chimes from my mother's anklet played too loudly in my head. The crows, too, made a lot of noise near the window where she always sat and prayed; there was no end to their cawing. I began to spend more time outside the house, trying hard to drown out the sounds.

MIRA

The sun shifted from the sky into my shorts and shoes. I was sitting on the branch closest to the ground, and though it was hurting my bum and I was sweating, I kept a straight face.

'Truth.'

I can say it fine now, but when I was four, maybe five, I couldn't say the word 'truth' properly, the same way I couldn't really say tomato and teeth and tongue. Other kids at school laughed. A couple of times Ma laughed. I don't really remember if Ashu did.

'Truth again? Alright,' Avni twisted her hair and put it in a small ponytail. 'What's the deal with your,' she raised her eyebrows, '*mom*?'

'What do you mean?' A line of red ants was crawling from the tree. One of the ants was trying to walk on my thigh. I thwacked it away.

'Well. My mom says she went a bit loopy after, you know, your dad.' Avni shrugged her shoulders.

'Loopy?' I asked.

She made a spiral with her finger next to her head. 'Loopy. Nuts. Mental?'

'That's not true! Ma is normal. Tell her, Ashu!'

Ashu looked at Avni lazily and said, 'Yeah. Ma is as normal as they come.'

'Haha,' said Avni. 'No, but seriously.'

Ashu and I exchanged a blank look.

'Are you serious?' Avni looked from Ashu to me, back again to Ashu. 'Do you really not know?' She let out a sharp laugh.

'Say something useful, Avni—or don't,' said Ashu.

Avni jumped off her branch and a cloud of dust went up in the air. 'Look, I was just saying it as it is. You can ignore me. My dad says I have a bad habit. Either I don't talk at all or I can't stop talking until my foot is in my mouth, you know. It's a family thing. My mom talks a lot, too.'

I tried to imagine Avni twisting her body and putting her foot inside her mouth, one toe at a time. She dropped the subject.

When it was Ashu's turn, he picked Truth, too.

'You have to pick something else. You're not eight. Come on, I dare you.' Avni narrowed her eyes.

Ashu shrugged. 'Okay.'

'Hmmmm,' Avni wiggled her fingertips together like a villain on TV before he goes muhahaha. She looked towards me. 'What dare shall we give him?'

I suggested that he should do a thousand jumping jacks.

Avni yawned and drilled her eyes on me. 'Really? Boring.' Except she said it like she was saying two words. Bo Ring.

'Fine. Then you give your own idea.'

Avni thought for a bit, then suddenly said, 'I know!' She turned to Ashu, 'Your dare is—to give me a kiss.'

'*What?*' Both Ashu and I spat.

'I can't do that!' Ashu sat up straight. 'We're cousins.'

'Splsfth.' Avni made a strange sound. 'Hardly. We've never met before now, have we?'

Avni made a good point and I said that to Ashu.

He looked pale in his face like all the colour in it had blown into the wind.

'Alright—' he went over to Avni and gave her a kiss on her cheek. Then he quickly sat down.

Avni said, 'This doesn't count. A proper one.'

She held Ashu's hand and made him get up again. 'Be right back.'

Ashu said nothing and followed her.

I waited there squinting my eyes at the sun for a long time. Flies buzzed in the sky and the hot air slapped my face. I didn't know what Avni and Ashu were up to. What was a proper kiss? The one that Ma gave me right on my ear which was very, very loud? Or did they mean the one that people gave each other in the movies—on the lips? In school people said that when you really love someone you spit into their mouth so they know that they are yours forever. I really hoped Ashu was not doing that. I hoped Ma and Coach never did that.

After five minutes, Avni came back alone from behind the grove of trees.

'Your brother is a scaredy cat. He didn't do anything,' she said and plonked herself on the ground. Ashu had run away and gone to where Ma was.

Of course he didn't, I thought, wiping the sweat from my face. He only likes Rahul.

ASHU

A few years ago, Ma had gone to the bank on a rainy day and didn't come to pick Ashu and Mira up from school. Ashu was nine years old then, and his sister four. Ashu noticed that it was the kind of monsoon day when long, brown earthworms gave up their introverted tendencies and punctuated the ground. He waited under an awning, which on less gloomy days protected the school security guard from heatstroke, and held Mira's hand. When a classmate's mother eventually noticed Ashu, and dropped him and Mira home, Ashu noticed Ma standing next to an unfamiliar man. Ma introduced the man to the children by his name, which was rare, then held his hand instead of Mira's, which was never.

That man was taller than anyone Ashu had ever met. The men in the marketplace his mother dragged him to tended to look shrunken, their backs curving in like they couldn't carry their own weight. This man, however, towered over them, straight-backed and tall like the mango trees Ashu and Mira so often played under, and instantly, Ashu felt a sense of calm. This one was going to be their father, he grinned to himself as he tried to trace patterns with the raindrops on the windowpane that afternoon. He was going to stay.

Ma often went out on dates with him, leaving Ashu and Mira at Mrs Shome's. Sometimes, he came over, and all four of them sat on the same sofa in a row, like pickle jars on a shelf. He made Ma laugh, and when she laughed her eyes crinkled up the same way Ashu's did when he tried to look at the sun. Then one day, the man came home with a suitcase. He lay it flat on the floor in Ma's bedroom and methodically removed one crisp starchy shirt after another and passed them to Ashu who placed them in the cupboard. Ashu had never seen the inside of a man's bag. There was not much in it besides a few plain shirts, a kit (black), a perfume in a glass container, which smelt of pencil shavings and the earth when it rained. A sunscreen bottle with its belly bloated; a single comb, its bristles new. There was also a pair of brown shoes with a tiny scuff on the side. When the man wasn't around, Ashu slipped into his shoes, saw briefly how small his own feet were in comparison. Ashu's toes barely made it halfway through the shoes, and he nearly fell trying to get out of them when he heard the door reopening.

In the nights, Ashu would be able to hear sounds through the wall. It was a dull sort of knocking that started and stopped without a discernible pattern. When Ashu first heard them, he imagined there were ghosts in the wall that whispered and conspired and spoke about secrets he longed to know. He shuffled out of bed, waking Mira up in the process, and sleepy-eyed, holding hands, they both tiptoed to Ma's room, where the ghosts seemed to be having a spectral conference. As they glued their small ears to the rough wooden door, fear and excitement twisted a knot in their stomachs and they waited for the courage to step in and save Ma. Then Ashu heard him. *Leela*, he said in a low raspy voice. *Leela*. And Ma made the sound you make when you stub your toe under the door. Ashu grabbed Mira's hand and ran back to their room. They had heard something they shouldn't have, he was sure, even though he didn't know what.

One afternoon, Ashu was playing hide-and-seek with Mira. The game was a farce, something he did as a favour to his sister. Most of the time, playing with Mira meant playing for her. Finding her was easy in most cases; she was always behind the bathroom door and squealed with delight and fear even before she was found. If she ever chose an innovative place to hide, it would be behind the drapes, light and flowing and patterned with leaves, and her little feet would always peek out from below. But that afternoon, when Ashu went to draw the curtain back, he found that Mira had planted her shoes there. She had tricked him; it was time for him to step up his game. Taking his younger sister for granted was his mistake. Ashu let out an excited burst of laughter, happy to find a worthy opponent to play with at last. He racked his brain, a manic energy in him now. There was a heightened sense of competition as they took turns in finding each other, their hiding places getting more and more uncommon. The only unsaid rule was not to hide in Ma's room.

'I'm coming, Ashuuu...' Mira shouted across the house, and his palms started getting sweaty. Beads formed on his neck, on his upper lip where in a few years faint markings of a moustache would grow. Time was slipping, and Ashu still hadn't found a place to hide. He placed his hand on the cool handle of Ma's door and entered.

The room from underneath Ma's bed looked different. He had scrambled to hide there, and now he saw that the cupboards seemed giant, bigger than he had ever imagined. The walls seemed to extend upwards endlessly, as though they had lost their manners and had forgotten to stop where the roof began. When he looked down to the floor, Ashu found whirls of dust that had bunched together, and he held in a strong desire to cough. Near the dust ball was a stray black pin Ma used to tie her hair with. He had seen these bunched up together on Ma's dressing table on a small glass plate with a gold rim. They clinked against the glass and made a special sound twice a day. Even underneath the bed, as Ashu touched the pin, he remembered how he had once tried to weave it through his own rough hair to see how it worked. The metal had ended up scratching his scalp and hurting it. Now, he threw it as far away from himself as he could.

'Ashoooo...'

Mira was calling out to him, but he could tell that she was confused, going in a completely different direction, maybe even towards the kitchen.

Ashu stifled a laugh and twisted his hands together.

Then the doorbell rang, and a gruff voice spoke. Suddenly, Ashu realised that this was a bad idea. Ma would be mad at Ashu in front of the man for playing in her room. And then he wouldn't like Ashu anymore.

Ashu pushed his arms on the floor and tried to wriggle his body out.

But the bedroom door opened and he saw shoes, brown, laced up, and he stayed where he was. Ma turned off the lights, and Ashu felt the world getting smaller, the roof of the bed moving closer towards him. When he saw Ma's printed dress drop to the floor in a heap, he wondered momentarily if she was going to take a bath again. From the shadows on the wall, Ashu saw the man inch closer towards Ma and their outlines became one. He waited with his breath stuck in his throat, counted to ten. Although he tried to think of something else, all he could imagine were trees rapidly whooshing over his head. The room seemed to shrink. The last thing he saw was a shadow of a hand going to Ma's face, slapping her like she had done something bad.

When Ashu woke up, the room was quiet. He slithered out from beneath the bed and got out of the room as quietly as he could. Ma was sitting in the corner of the living room. Her shoulders were shaking. Ashu ran into the bathroom, splashed water on his face and took huge gulps of air to help him breathe.

The next day, when the man came over, he brought cake for Ashu and Mira. The meaner he was to Ma, Ashu noticed, the nicer he was afterwards. This happened a few times. Once, he even offered to help Ashu learn to drive. Ma didn't say anything; her back was turned to them and she was looking outside the window. Ashu was only eight years old and his feet could barely touch the floor of the car. But the man insisted, 'You're going to be a big boy soon!' When he held Ashu's hands and guided them into the ten and two position, Ashu felt his face turn hot, like he was the direct target of the sun, the sole reason it burned.

Later at night, he watched his retreating figure as he walked into Ma's room, met her there, his fingers entwined around hers, not unlike the way his fingers clutched the driving stick.

A few weeks passed, during which time Ashu oscillated between guilt and desire, a feeling of helplessness and a kind of happiness that was incomparable to all the ways he had felt in the past. Just when he believed he could reconcile all these new emotions, Ma announced one morning at the breakfast table, her face pale, that the man wasn't going to come over anymore.

That night was one of the last times Ma allowed Ashu to sleep in her bed. Mira was there too. Ashu had coiled himself into a ball. Strangely, the bed still smelt like the man—a little like leather and a little like the rain, but when Ashu cuddled into Ma, all he could smell was the baby powder that Ma liked to use. Even though Ma's silk nightie stuck to Ashu's skin and his elbow hurt from the angle it was at, he didn't want to move. They were there, they were together. That was enough. There was a window right above Ma's cupboard. The glass was smudged and hazy because Ma always said that there was no point cleaning a window like that—there was nothing much to see from it anyway. Still, lying there with his arm crooked, next to Ma and Mira, Ashu could see a little orange square of sky. It started raining, and the colours shifted quickly to red and pink and back to orange. It was a day without rules, and the sky was growing brighter and brighter. Ashu hoped that the sky wouldn't change its mind. That instead of turning into night, it would retrace its steps and slide back into day. Or, at least, that it would stay that way forever, the trees moving slightly, the fan just so, all of them sleeping and smiling like nothing bad could ever happen to them again.

How to Get (Accidentally) Pregnant:

Go on a date with a man because you can't stand to be in a house whose walls now shake with grief. Sneak out quietly, rapidly, eagerly. Ignore the thumps of unease in your heart. Your bangs swish across your face, and you carry on. You haven't learnt any better. You've stolen a denim skirt from your sister's cupboard that makes your skinny bum look round and plush. It suits you, you like it. And let's be honest—you've always been the better-looking one anyway. Meet your date—your friend's boyfriend—by the corner of the road. The plan? To drive around in the dark and listen to the newest Simon & Garfunkel album.

But you'll notice that the friend's boyfriend doesn't have the tape or any good tapes at all in his car. And if he is smoking a cigarette with you and blowing puffs of smoke into your skinny bangs, he's probably your boyfriend, right? Your boyfriend—you shudder in excitement or sickness at the word—will start to drive faster. You'll cross your legs because that's what they do in the novels you read. You'll make a casual, witty remark or two. You'll say, 'Slow down there, cowboy' with a nervous laugh. It'll sound vaguely sexy, enough to do the trick, and he'll bring the car to a screeching halt and park it under a tree. He'll tug at the denim skirt and tell you that you both know why you are here. You do, but you'll suddenly feel nervous. Though you have to keep up the image you've maintained so far, so you'll say, of course. Of Course. Then it'll begin.

He'll slide into you, a cock bigger than you thought possible because you had always imagined them like punctured balloons—limp and flat. He'll pound in and out. And in and out. You've heard that this is meant to be pleasurable, but it'll feel like a rubber pump extracting water. Mechanical and rote. Painful. You'll want it to stop. You'll say so in the middle, but he'll take it as a challenge and push harder. You'll say it again, but when he covers your mouth with his hands, you'll learn that protesting is futile. You'll keep your mouth shut. When he's done, he'll zip his pants up and drop you off at your house. Before leaving, he'll brush his hand on your cheek and remind you not to mention this to your friend. You'll nod and say that he doesn't have to worry about it. You'll never mention it to anyone at all.

MIRA

When I open my eyes tomorrow morning, I'll be nine. What Ashu and Ma and Avni don't realise—even though I've told them many times—is that even today, I'm a little nine. Like when I turned seven, I was a big seven and a little eight. And when I turned six, I became a big six and a small seven. Today, because there is a whole day left for my birthday, I am a big eight and a little nine. And finally, tomorrow, when I jump out of bed and run to the wall where we mark our height, I will be fully nine. No more eight. And even a small ten. And I will grow taller, taller, even taller than Ashu and Rahul. That's what happens in your sleep before your birthday.

When I explained this to Ma again today, she glanced at me while reading the newspaper and said, 'That's funny, Mira. Never seen you this captivated by numbers.'

I remembered my maths marks and gulped.

'She isn't right though,' Ashu said, twisting his lips. 'It's a stupid idea.'

Even Avni laughed at me. She said that I would remain stuck at eight years old forever because I think silly things like these.

Two days ago, we came back home from our holiday. We were all tired and slept the whole way on the car ride back. Obviously not Ma because she was driving and she couldn't. I was sleeping so much that I didn't even get to know when the blue sky had turned grey and the tiny shops with too many words on them had turned into homes. We stopped at McDonald's again, and this time I didn't ask any questions about periods or anything. Before we got back into the car, Ma went to the bathroom and stayed there for ten minutes. When she returned, she looked happy but smelt burnt.

From the day we got home, we've been eating the mangoes we brought back from the farm. One for breakfast, two for lunch and three for dinner. I could eat only mangoes forever and ever because mangoes are the best fruit in the world. So far we've had mango ice cream and mango lassi, which is Ashu's favourite. Mrs Shome also made us mango sandesh, which is a white sweet with a small mango blanket wrapped around it. I like biting into mangoes and making them go drip-drip on my clothes, but I have to run and wash the juice off before Ma can see it. Ashu also eats mangoes like me, all messy, but he's a lot better at sitting in funny shapes and not letting the juice spill onto his clothes. He's had much more practice than me because he is older. I will become better at it too. When I am thirteen, I will:

1. Hide mango stains from Ma like a mango expert
2. Grow my hair long and swishy
3. Have my own best friend at school with whom I can walk around—with my arm around their shoulder
4. Be asked to give someone a proper kiss EXCEPT I will obviously say no

At first there were seven people at my birthday party. Me, Ma, Ashu, Rahul, Mrs Shome, Avni, and Mausi, who was returning the next day from her work trip to take Avni home with her. Ma asked me if I wanted to call someone from school, but I told her that everyone was away for summer holidays. Ma gave me a funny glance which meant that she didn't believe me, but thankfully she didn't say anything more. While we were wrapping return presents for the party, she went to talk on the phone in her room, and when she came back, she looked like she was hiding a smile. 'Your party is getting bigger,' Ma said. 'There's an addition to the guest list.'

'Who?' I got a weird feeling in my stomach. I really hoped it wasn't Mrs Dubey. And more than that, I really, really hoped it wasn't—

'Coach.' Ma scratched the side of her thumb with her nail.

'Coach?' I groaned, but Ma gave me a Look.

It doesn't make me too happy that Coach is coming, but maybe it's better than having a schoolteacher at your birthday party. I said OK.

Later, when Ma wasn't around, Ashu asked me, 'What do you think?'

I told him I was wondering if Coach would wear his whistle to my birthday party too.

I stayed awake till so late that night, I could hear the dogs on the street shouting *a-wooo* like wolves in the forest. They sounded like they were wishing me a happy birthday. What would Ma say if I told her that I wanted to invite them to the party too? They could be my friends. They could wear party hats and sit on chairs. They could bring me presents and give me birthday bumps. But what if they began licking the cake too? I decided I didn't want to invite the wolf-dogs after all, so I pulled the blanket over my head and went to sleep.

When I woke up, I ran to the wall to see if I had become taller, but somehow I was the same. Everyone, including Mausi, who had just come from the airport, was getting things ready for the party. Mrs Shome was in the kitchen helping Ma cook the food. They were making all my favourite things to eat like colourful fryums and mini pizzas and noodles and biryani. Usually I only get to eat them sometimes, and separately, but on my birthday I get to eat them all on one day together.

Ma was making jalebi, and her face was all sweaty from drawing circles round and round in the oil. She kept splashing oil from the big spoon onto the circles and the batter danced and jumped until the jalebis became nice and sweet and golden and crunchy. Then she fished one out and popped it into my mouth. It was hot. Very hot. But I didn't want to make Ma mad, so I said Thank you! with my jalebi teeth and jalebi tongue.

Just when I had gulped it down, Mausi gave me a gift wrapped with a bow. I tore it open before Ma could take it away. It was a T-shirt. Clothes are the most boring gifts you can get, but it's rude to say that, so I said that I loved it. But maybe Mausi knew that I didn't really mean it because she said, 'It's a glow-in-the-dark T-shirt! It shines when you wear it in a dark room. All the kids your age love them.' Her eyes sparkled.

'Go on then, try it.' Ma waved her hand in the air.

I went running to the bathroom, and I could hear Mausi saying to Ma behind me, 'Just picked it up at the airport. It was nothing.'

I changed out of the blue dress I was wearing and tried the glow-in-the-dark T-shirt with shorts instead. It still looked a bit boring. Remembering what Mausi said, I offed the light, and suddenly I looked like a firefly. It was the opposite of boring. If I wore the T-shirt and stood in the dark, all of me disappeared—like the tip of my nose, my ears, my short hair and the marks on my elbow from the time that I fell off a cycle—and all you could see were the stars and butterflies on the tee. If I wore this to school, I would make at least two new friends who'd ask me about it. And because I'd want them to be my friends, I wouldn't be snooty and lift my nose to the ceiling but would say, 'You can borrow it anytime.' And when people would ask where I got it from, I'd say that my Mausi gave it to me, which is true because now I have one.

At the party, I sat squeezed on the sofa between Avni and Ashu. I asked Ashu if he'd seen my T-shirt glow in the dark, but he was scowling at something and said no. When I turned to Avni, she told me the T-shirt was for babies and she was only helping me by telling me I should not wear it.

Since the game on the trip, Avni had become my friend because she was mad at Ashu for not kissing her. She had started playing with me and talking to me. She even looked pointedly at Ashu and whispered secrets into my ear. For instance, she told me that she had a boyfriend back home whom she had left hanging. He had proposed to her by giving her a ring.

'What ring?' I asked.

She showed me. It was HUGE and pink and a little small for her finger, and it proved that he really loved her.

'If you tell my mom or yours, I'll stop talking to you,' Avni warned me, so of course I told nobody. She even told me that she had seen her boyfriend's *thing*, and when I asked her why she'd want to do that, she scoffed and said that I was such a child.

Actually, one time, when we were smaller, I saw a *thing* too. It was Ashu's, and I looked at it by accident when he was coming out of the bathroom, and he ran away putting his hand in front of him. I laughed at him so much that even Ma, who is usually on my side, told me to shut up.

The grown-ups were all talking amongst themselves and playing loud music, so I started thinking about what wish I would make when I blew out the candles on my cake. Last week, Mrs Shome had asked me what flavour of cake I wanted, and because I couldn't decide between chocolate and strawberry, in the end she made me a chocolate-strawberry cake with swirls around the middle.

She wrote my name on it too. M I R A. It's lucky that my name is short and can fit on a cake because there are some people whose names are so long that they would run out of cake and fall onto the floor.

Mrs Shome also got me a big book of facts about the world. She said, 'This will go well with the globe.' Ashu and I looked down sheepishly, and our eyes darted to the cupboard of useless things, hoping she wouldn't open it and feel bad.

I kept thinking about my wish because you only get one chance to do it and it only comes once a year. I've tried pushing my face forward on Ashu's birthdays and adding a little wish when he is cake-blowing. But it doesn't work that way. You need to do it on your own birthday, that's the rule. I was waiting to cut my cake, but there were still two guests missing. One was Rahul.

His mother had called before the party to say that he would come late. Ashu sat around moping ever since as though it were Rahul's birthday and not mine, which was annoying. Even right now, Ashu had his chin on his hand as if he were listening to me. He seemed grumpy the way I do sometimes when I'm hungry. 'Are you sure you don't want to see my—?' I asked him again, but the doorbell rang, and Ashu looked away.

ASHU

Ashu was sure it was Rahul. It had to be Rahul. Because Rahul's mother had called earlier to say that they had all just reached home from his Nani's—that they were stopping by his father's office and coming. And his father's office was about twenty minutes away from Rahul's house, and Ashu's home was fifteen minutes away from there. It had to be Rahul because Ashu had been keeping track of time ever since the phone call came, even though Mira was making it hard to focus and kept going on and on about something next to him. He could swear that birthdays were not only making her older but also more annoying.

But it was only Coach, as it turned out, whose balding head first appeared as he entered the doorframe, followed by a bright floral shirt and—Ashu wondered if it were meant to be a fashion statement—a beaded necklace slung around his neck. Biting back a laugh and a nagging feeling of frustration, Ashu caught Mira's eye, who too was looking aghast at Coach's outfit.

Ma, who was near the door, puffed up her hair and said, 'Well, Coach, don't you look festive today.'

Coach laughed and leaned towards Ma, whispering something in her ear, close to the spot where Ma had a birthmark. Laughing as if she had heard the funniest thing in the world, Ma moved away and let him in.

'The club misses you two!' Coach walked towards Ashu now and ruffled the back of his head. Then he shook Mira's hand and handed her a gift bag.

Ashu, close to Mira, took a peek inside. The bag was full of chocolates. 'Better than a swimsuit and goggles,' Ashu heard Mira giggling into his ear.

Despite himself, Ashu laughed. He had been holding out on Mira, but something softened in him. He threw her a bait. 'You're becoming funnier, silly goose.'

He saw Mira puff up with pride. 'Now do you want to—' she began to murmur something, but his attention shifted towards the door. Everyone started looking at Rahul. But Rahul only looked at him.

* * *

Sitting between Rahul and Avni at the party, Ashu realised for the first time that this was the most awkward situation he had ever been in. And that was saying something, since he had felt awkward for most of his life.

'So I was saying—' Avni continued in a loud, affected voice, '—it was amazing there. Just so *serene*, you know?'

Ashu suppressed an urge to remind Avni that the entire time they were at the farm, she had complained about the dust, her white pants getting dirty, her nails coming off (which Ashu thought was an alarming cause for concern, but Avni seemed pretty offhand about it), and the weather. But now she went on about the pleasures of rural living, bobbing her head vigorously the whole while. While Avni had been distant with Ashu after the farm visit, once Rahul arrived at the party she seemed to like him again.

Rahul couldn't get a word in edgeways, but he tried.

Now, putting his arm around Ashu, he said, 'Ash doesn't mind being back though, does he?' He smiled.

Ashu felt his ears going hot.

'Well,' Avni stopped short. 'You can't be too sure about that.'

Ashu buried his head into his palms. It was a strange situation, but it seemed to be slipping out of control even as he watched it happen. Avni and Rahul, from completely different parts of his world, had been placed together and seemed to be fighting over him. They were so different—and who Ashu was with each of them was so different too—that he felt split asunder, unable to choose which version of himself to be. To be silent and slightly dismissive of Avni as he tended to be; to be sarcastic and playful with Rahul like he was when they were alone. Or was he to be Mira's older brother—who was gentle, and looked out for her, took care of her, sometimes even when he didn't want to?

Around them, the room started getting noisier. In one corner of the room Ashu saw Mira being spun round and round by Mrs Shome. Ma, Mausi and Coach, too, were occupied. They each had a glass in their hands, and Ashu didn't have to guess what those contained. Coach had taken over the floor and was narrating some sort of an anecdote. It was funny, apparently, or at least Ma thought so, for she couldn't stop laughing. Ashu had noticed that there were two kinds of men. The kinds who got loud when they drank, as if this was their only chance to speak, to tell their stories, to be heard. And the kinds who got really quiet, like everything inside their body and mind had dimmed to a single source of light that very moment. Ashu supposed there was a third kind too—men who did not drink. But he hadn't met anybody like that.

Ashu suddenly felt exhausted and began to wish he wasn't at the party. That the room would shrink, taking in everything, and it would be just him and Rahul on the terrace—or him and Mira, inside their room, exchanging fart noises. Or even just him, by himself, and there was nothing more comfortable.

So, when Avni asked him if he wanted to get fresh air, he jumped at the idea.

'Hold on,' he said to her and Rahul both. 'I'll just be back.'

He snuck into Ma's room, which seemed to him now like a safe haven from the party. He closed the door behind him and the sounds from the living room retreated. He took a deep breath and relished the moment of quiet away from all the people, before beginning to look. He was sure Ma would have it hidden somewhere. He looked under Ma's mattress, then in her bedside drawers. The back of her wardrobe, the cabinet in the bathroom. He thought finally to check the cupboard of unwanted things and tugged at its handle as quietly as he could. Despite his best efforts, the cupboard flung open with a loud thwang. As Ashu began to rummage through the dark spaces in the cupboard, little things fell from the shelf: dusty birthday cards, a sewing box, a notebook, an old tin of peppermints that had long expired, and finally, a dented white carton of cigarettes. He grabbed the box and shoved it into his pocket. He took a breath, holding on to the cool metal handle for a moment longer, then opened the door.

MIRA

'I know what you're doing,' I said.

Coach, who was eating a slice of cake, had been sitting alone, so I had gone and slouched into the plastic chair next to him. I had looked around and seen no other grown-ups. There was no time to waste.

'What am I doing, kid?'

'Making my Ma a whore.'

Coach nearly spat out the cake in his mouth. 'Do you know what, uh, that word means, kid?'

What did he think I was? Eight? I stared at him fiercely. 'Of course. I read it in a book.'

This was a lie. Actually I had heard it in school when some older kids had used it, and later I had looked it up in the dictionary.

Coach stared at me.

I realised he wanted me to tell him what it meant.

'Well—' I cleared my throat to say it in the nicest way possible. 'It means that you want to give her a kiss in exchange for swimming lessons. You're trying to trap her.' I imagined Coach's face in place of the spider in our room and him trying to catch Ma in the web.

Coach laughed, and for some reason he looked relieved. 'Kid, of course not. I'm your Ma's, uh, friend. You know she doesn't have too many of those. You don't want your Ma to be lonely. Do you?'

I thought about this. It was bad enough that I had only one friend, Avni, and that was also because she had asked Ashu to kiss her and Ashu had said No way. It would be worse if Ma lost her friends too. Especially because she has no ring on her left finger and no black-and-gold necklace around her neck which everyone at school says grown-ups should wear, otherwise they're sad. So, I muttered, 'Ok fine. You can be her friend.'

He stretched his plate out and offered me some of his cake.

I had already eaten two pieces of cake and ten jalebis when Ma wasn't looking, and now my tummy was rumbling like there was lightning in it. Thankfully, no one could hear it because of the music that was playing. I said No, but thank you anyway.

Ma popped her head around the kitchen door, 'Can I get you anything, Coach? Something more to drink? Maybe a—?' She did an action with her finger I didn't understand.

'No, nothing, thanks!' Coach lifted up the glass he had in his hand to show Ma. 'Please carry on.'

'Alright,' said Ma and she went back into the kitchen. I saw Avni, Ashu and Rahul disappearing around the corner. Where were they going? Maybe they were going outside to get me something?

Coach looked at me and said, 'Now that I have your permission, maybe we can be friends too?' He was eating the cake in big mouthfuls and making loud chewing noises. When Ashu or I do that, Ma lifts her hand and smacks it on our thighs. Are you cows? Going nohm-nohm-nohm-nohm like that? If we laugh, she smacks harder and says that it's not funny and no one will talk to us if we eat like this.

I felt bad. Maybe no one had told Coach that you aren't supposed to eat like a cow in public.

I decided to be a grown-up, despite Coach's disgusting eating habits. I said, 'Ok. We can be friends. But you have to tell me one thing.'

Ma and Mausi were arguing over who would get to wash the dishes and who bought what. The sounds of plates clattering and glasses toppling were coming from the kitchen.

'What?' Coach smiled. There were bits of pink icing decorating the front of his teeth. He closed his mouth.

'What's your real name? Everyone keeps calling you Coach.'

He raised his palms up like he was praying to the skies and laughed. 'That's a secret! I can't tell you that easily now.'

'Why not?' I stuck out my chin.

'I'll tell you if you give me something in return.'

'Like a return present?' I asked.

'Exactly! You're a, uh, smart kid.'

'Because I'm not a kid, I'm nine.' It was annoying that I had to keep reminding people.

He looked around the room. I thought hard about what I could say to him so he would tell me his real name. Then I got the idea.

'I can show you magic. It's very cool!'

Coach looked at me like he didn't believe me.

'Do you want to see a shirt that glows in the dark?'

'Glows in the dark? That's, uh, impossible!' he said, but his face was beaming.

'I can show you if you don't believe me. Here.' I tried to cover my T-shirt with my arms. 'Can you see?'

Coach shook his head. 'It won't work like this. You have to switch off the, uh, light.'

I looked at him doubtfully. Ma would scold me if I made the living room dark during the party. I said so.

'Maybe your room?' he said and looked towards the balcony.

The grown-ups had now shifted from the kitchen and were drinking their juice there.

It was a good idea. I started walking out of the living room, and because Coach was getting up too slowly, I stretched the end of a word like chewing gum: 'Come with meeeeeee.'

He followed me to the room Ashu and I shared. All the lights were on, so my T-shirt still looked ordinary and even a little bit boring.

I hurried to explain. 'When I make it dark, this will sparkle like fireflies. And you'll have to tell me your name.'

Coach nodded and licked his teeth, scraping the icing onto his tongue.

I offed the light near the bed. It was so black in the room now that the only things I could see were Coach's white laces, his lemon-yellow teeth as he said Wow! and the butterflies on my T-shirt that were flying and glittering in the dark.

He cleared his throat and did a single cough, then said, 'But I need to see it better. Come here?'

Coach patted the bottom bunk. He put his arm around my waist and pulled me to the bed. But when I sat down, it was not the bed, it was Coach's lap.

My heart was now making loud thump-thump sounds inside my ear. It was too dark. Was I going to get my first proper kiss? I didn't want it.

I said to Coach, 'I have to go. Ma is calling me.'

'No one's calling. Let me see the butterfly, baby.'

He put his hand on my T-shirt and his fingers went hop hop hop on all the butterflies that were glowing. I felt something in the bottom of my stomach like I did when I by mistake watched grown-up TV on a Saturday morning. I squeezed my thighs together like an ice cream sandwich. I didn't like what he was doing. I liked what he was doing. Coach's lap squirmed underneath me. He put his other hand on my back and began to rub it slowly like Ma does when she's drawing shapes on me. A kidney bean, the earth, no, the sun, I thought automatically as he traced his fingers slowly on my back. Except I love it when Ma does it. I didn't like this at all. I jumped off his lap and ran out of the room. The dark stole my butterflies and they vanished from my T-shirt as I ran towards the light. Ma and the grown-ups were walking back from the balcony laughing at something loudly.

I almost collided with Ma. 'Hold your horses, birthday girl,' she said. Then she saw Coach, who was walking fast-fast from my room to the balcony.

Ma had a big question mark on her face. I wondered if she could read my mind, like the ads on TV do. But she just walked to the balcony. Coach was standing there with Mrs Shome and Mausi now, with a fresh glass in his hand. When Ma joined him, he laughed and squeezed her hand. I couldn't tell if Ma squeezed back.

Then Coach's phone rang, and he picked it up and went to the corner and talked.

Who was calling him? A police inspector who knew he'd done something bad? Kids from the pool? I couldn't guess.

All the grown-ups were talking to each other, but no one was asking about me or wondering where I was. I was glad. I didn't want to talk to them or tell them anything. If I told Ma, I would have to tell her about the grown-up TV and the feeling in my thighs when I pressed them together too tight, and she would say Yuck! you should go back to being eight. Or worse, she would say You should go back to being zero.

I walked outside the house to look for Ashu. Rahul and Avni and Ashu were standing underneath the gulmohar tree which, in the dark, looked like a giant mushroom standing over them.

Ashu coughed when he saw me and Avni thumped his back. As I walked over, all three of them started whispering to each other.

'Where were you?' I said, digging my shoes into the mud.

'Here.' Ashu and Rahul spoke at the same time and looked at each other shiftily.

'Doing what?' I looked around. There was nothing to do under the tree.

'We can only tell you if you're ten and above.' Avni lifted her nose up.

'She's kidding,' Ashu said. Then he looked at all three of us. 'Let's go back in.'

Ashu, Rahul and Avni began walking towards the house, and when I didn't follow, Ashu turned around and said, 'Why're you just standing there, silly goose? Come!'

Ashu has his secrets, but now that I'm nine, I have a big secret too. And I won't tell anyone at all. I'll keep the secret in my stomach, deep, deep down in the same place where I keep cake and bad feelings. I followed him and thought of telling him to go take a bath when the party got over. I couldn't sleep in the same room as him. Because Ashu was smelling just like Ma did sometimes.

Like black, black smoke.

ASHU

Mausi and Avni were leaving. Their suitcases were all packed and zipped up. The taxi had been called and the driver was waiting outside the house. He had his meter running, and every few minutes he spat out the red gutka from his mouth and honked to check if the passengers were coming. Ma shouted at him from the balcony and told him that he wouldn't get any extra money for his impatience. Usually a stern look from Ma was enough to shut people down.

Ma had suggested that she and Coach would drive Mausi and Avni to the airport. But Mausi insisted that she had put them all through too much trouble already. Had it been a month since the holidays had begun? Ashu could swear that it felt like a few days only since school had shut for the summer and they had begun swimming lessons.

Ashu believed that he could now divide his life neatly in two. Before summer, there had been only three people in his family, Ma, Mira and Ashu, with his name trailing behind just like he did in real life. After summer, Ashu found out that there were others whom he was related to by blood. That not only did Ma have a sister, but he, too, had a cousin, no matter how odd she was. Ashu couldn't help but wonder how many more people were going to come tumbling into their life, how many others Ma had kept hidden from them in a secret place.

Before summer, Ashu had felt lonely at home, but in a way that he assumed was normal for most people. Didn't everyone feel like they didn't understand the foreign language that the rest were speaking? After summer, he felt a distinct and palpable shift in his loneliness, especially when he was around Mausi or spending time with Avni. Like maybe there was a possibility that it was going to be taken away, and somehow that made him want to hold on to it a bit tighter.

And lastly, before this summer, Ashu had never kissed anyone. But now that the summer was dwindling to an end, he couldn't help but wonder what was going to happen. With Rahul back in town, Ashu could feel something, an excitement at the back of his knees, but he didn't quite know what to do with it.

There were so many things he kept hidden. Thoughts crystallised into secrets whenever he didn't say them. They became sharp, little icicles that hung from the roof of his mouth and they hurt him each time he slammed his lips shut to keep from saying unwanted things. When he saw Ma bring home a man who was bad, a small icicle grew. When Ma told him she'd iron his eyebrows because he raised them too much, an icicle grew. When he watched the news with Ma and saw people taken to jail for being different, another icicle grew. When he looked on as Ma hugged Mira for a little longer than him, it grew. Now that he was fourteen, he had a collection of these icicles, sharp and painful, a living museum of the things he wanted to ask and things he could never say.

Sometimes, he felt the icicles collapse briefly. It happened when he laughed under the sun with Rahul. Or when he walked home from the market alone, kicking stones out of his way, his pockets filled with sweets and a cigarette. But the moments would pass.

There was a time when Ashu was convinced that the pain was

real; he could feel these icicles growing, physically cutting through his gums. When it became too painful to ignore, he spoke to Mrs Shome who spoke to Ma. Ma had grabbed him by his arm and taken him to the dentist. The doctor had made a joke about why doughnuts went to the dentist (to get fillings!) that Ashu didn't find funny at all, thumped a cool metal appliance on his gums and pulled some sick teeth that were at the back of his mouth. Ashu had stared numbly as Ma handed over a wad of cash into the receptionist's palms, like she was embarrassed at how much she had to spend on Ashu. It was Mira who had held his hand during the process, her five tiny nails digging into his flesh.

Days later after the relief, Ashu felt it again—an insistent, gnawing pain in his mouth, but this time there were no teeth to blame and no dentists to go to. So he bit his tongue and held his quiet in.

* * *

The taxi driver outside honked once more, and this time, Ashu was the one who stuck his head out the window at home and shouted mildly, 'Please wait. We're coming!'

Inside the house, Coach was sitting on the sofa and eating onion pakoras, dipping them in ketchup, while Mausi looked around the home. She was shaking open drawers and instructing Avni to look under the bed. 'Wherever we go, Avni leaves at least one thing behind. And usually it's something she's stolen from my cupboard. This time it's my ring.' Avni had decided a few days ago that she wasn't satisfied with the plastic ring she had got with her from school. It was tacky, she had now decided and had taken her mother's. Ashu wanted to laugh when he saw that, partly because he didn't think that Avni even had a boyfriend, and if she did, he felt sorry for him.

Ashu looked closer at Mausi. She and Ma looked so similar, but there was something about Mausi that felt softer. Like looking at a reflection in a pool of water. Even her eyes were rounder.

There were times when Ma looked at Ashu as though she didn't know how she had birthed him. Like he was a science project gone wrong, a model volcano that erupted early and spoilt the sofa in the room, leaving a sour smell in the air for days. But when Mausi did something as little as passing a spoon to Ashu at the table, she looked at him, *really* looked at him.

Earlier this summer, Ashu had taken the landline into the bathroom, twisted the cord around his fingers and tried calling Rahul at his Nani's place, again and again and again. He had dialled the digits several times, repeating under his breath the new number Rahul had made him memorise, but each time it led to a blank dial tone. When Ashu eventually walked out of the bathroom, Ma stared at him. After Ma left, Mausi made a passing remark, 'Lucky girl,' and she winked at Ashu, making him feel loved, but at the same time, very alone.

Right now, Ashu shifted downstairs with their suitcases. He felt the sweat on his back mixing with the stench of pollution. He'd have to change his T-shirt later, he thought, maybe spray some deodorant to mask the smell before he went over to Rahul's. The cab driver kept shaking his leg, waiting impatiently. When Mausi and Avni finally arrived downstairs, the ring having been retrieved, the driver opened the black door of the car with a jerk, and Ashu noticed an awful red and orange flower print cover the taxi's ceiling. Suddenly, Ashu felt a heavy weight in his chest. How was it possible to feel like he was going to lose someone close when he hadn't even known of their existence until a few weeks ago? Mira went in to hug Avni and Mausi first, clinging to them as they hugged her back. Ma followed, reluctantly exchanging hugs with her sister. Then, Mausi said goodbye to Coach, who waved back at her.

Last, it was Ashu's turn. Like the first time she met him, Mausi pulled Ashu close for a hug. He was tempted to let his arms hang, to brush off her love like one brushes off a loose thread at the edge of the sofa. But he closed his eyes, and this time, when she came near, he put his arms around her, and only when the driver pressed the horn in impatience, did he let go.

SWIM

Some days Ma is like a butterfly. She is flying from room to room. She is running from home to office. She is going out for dinner and making us clean the house fast fast. She plays the globe game and the how-was-your-day game and the guessing game and all the games in the world one can play. She is shiny and colourful and her eyes are bright. She reads ten books at a time and moves so fast that she is like superwoman, and I have to say Maa stop! I can't see you! but she is flying everywhere and can't stop, won't stop.

But some days, like today, Ma is a moth. She is black, she is dark. She still moves from home to office and school but she moves slowly. She looks a little bit like me and Ashu in the morning when we're sleepy, except I don't think Ma is sleepy. Ma is just sluggish. She sits still in her bed for hours and watches the TV even though the TV is not working properly. Maybe Ma doesn't even need a TV to work to watch it. She just has to think of the movie name that she wants to watch and it goes pop! and starts playing inside her head. That's because she is bigger and has also seen many more movies than me. So that's why she can watch them in her head, that's the rule. I want a TV head too. Sometimes I imagine twisting my hair up like an antenna reaching the sky so that I can catch the signal, but sooner rather than later my ponytail falls, and no TV comes.

On the days that Ma is not Madame Butterfly but is Sire Moth, she is smelly. She doesn't take a bath and doesn't put on perfume from the small bottle that fits in the palm of her hand and makes her smell like honey. She doesn't tell me and Ashu to take a bath either, which I don't mind, especially on those days that it's so cold outside that our teeth go brrrrrrrr. She doesn't say anything to Ashu when he shakes his leg under the dining table so much that it feels like the earth is quaking around us. She doesn't even say anything to me when I make my hair wet from the tap and shape it all spiky like the top of a pineapple.

She picks up a book and forgets to flip the page. She takes us to school but forgets to turn the wheel. Sometimes she even forgets to cook, but Ashu knows how to make a yummy cheese sandwich—with corners cut the way I like it—and he makes one for himself and one for me for school. If I start to get worried and cry about Ma and her Moth Days, he says shush, puts one arm around me and tells me to wait. Don't worry, silly, he says. Wait for a couple of days.

He is right. Ma's Moth Days only stay for a while. No one knows when and why they come. But we know they always go.

When I first told my father about my decision, his jaw bulged like a frog's so much that I nearly called up my sister to laugh.

'Are you sure?' he asked.

My father didn't sound like himself. Then again, I had no idea what he sounded like before my mother died. It had always seemed as though their marriage had a specific word limit, and my mother had taken claim of the whole share. He barely talked. If my mother demanded, he contributed with a grunt or a nod. With her gone, he had lost the only language he knew. He began to rely on the movies he watched for support, repeating phrases and words he had heard through the screen. Is anybody home? What's for dinner? Are you sure?

I stared at my hands. I hadn't realised I had been wringing them, twisting my fingers like wet laundry.

Even though there were fewer of us living in our house than ever before, the air in it had become damp, suffocating. My sister, who was now married, stayed away as though our grief would enter her new life and infect her happiness. My father began feebly, and unsuccessfully, to take on the duties of the house. He rang the ghanti of the puja room, but his hands shook, so the ringing of the bell sounded offbeat. He cooked dal-chawal, but it was all wrong—too salty, too little rice. He took to fixing leaks in the bathroom, to straightening paintings that were horizontal already. Nothing worked. Home repairs couldn't distract him from the fact that his wife was dead.

I wondered many times if I should borrow my father's pain. I felt it radiating from him strongly, even in that moment when I told him what I wanted to do. I could extend my finger and lightly touch his grief and borrow some. But what would be the conditions attached to this loan? Would the pain expand with interest? Would it compound? When would I be able to return it? Or would it be indefinite, the burden of my mother's death on me, claiming all of my life, while my father would suddenly try to break free? I couldn't deal with these uncertainties, so I didn't take them.

Then one day, it arrived as a shock to the stomach, a punch to the gut. I had been zipping down my pants several times, waiting since it usually came like clockwork. I was searching for a hint of blood; I imagined every movement in my lower body to be the onset of my period. When a few days passed, I sneaked out to the pharmacy, where a few months ago I had smoked a pack a day, and I bought a kit. The double lines were clearly visible. I couldn't fool myself if I tried.

Later, when I went to my father to tell him that I wanted to get married—that I missed my mother too much—and I didn't really mind who I got married to as long as he was a good person, he was surprised at my decision. I had evaded for so long his insistence that I marry, that now when the words came from me he began to second-guess the idea himself.

'Are you sure?' he asked once more. He sounded almost sad. Again, there were the words that didn't belong to him. Again, his grief, quivering, close enough for me to touch, hold.

I nodded and stepped away.

* * *

'He-hello?' His voice came through the phone.

I didn't have a minute to waste. I came straight to the point. 'Do you want to meet?'

When we met at the tea shop, plates of chicken momos lay untouched between us as I told him everything but one essential truth. I said that I liked him. I was keen to get married, and I was wrong to refuse his offer before. It wasn't the same with my mother gone, and things were strange with my sister too. That I realised by letting go of him, I'd be letting go of a very good option. That my father agreed it was a good idea. That my mother would have too.

At this point in my life, I looked mildly attractive. Men tended to like you if you liked yourself, so I had begun to give off an air of confidence that I didn't even know I had. All it took was a flick of the hair, a finality in tone, a surety in step, and they lapped it all up like lions at the watering hole.

But he wasn't like that. I knew when I was talking, he was actually listening to me, not staring at my cleavage. I knew when he drove, unlike some men, he didn't purposely make the car jump over the speedbump so that my breasts would bounce and he could sneak a look. He listened to my speech with searing sincerity. He ignored the sounds from the other tables near us and gazed at me, like he did that day in my living room, as though he really wanted to know me. We sipped our milky tea and ate the momos, and something punched me in the gut again; I wanted to throw up. I held in the bile and whispered lies instead.

He held my hand that day, his fingers touching mine. He noticed the bit of skin on my thumb that I had pulled too hard with my teeth a few weeks ago after grazing it against the rough edge of a library bookshelf. It bled. When he asked me what had happened, I shrugged and bit my lip. He rubbed his thumb over the skin, smoothing it back down. I smiled. No one had ever looked at me like that before. After him, no one looked at me like that again.

* * *

The wedding date was set for a month later. Khushbu dropped her copy of A Suitable Boy *and split the 1349-page tome by its seams when she heard. 'We thought you'd be the last one of us,' she said. It was true. I had always claimed that I was above things like marriage, that it would be the last of my priorities. But now, I smiled wryly as if to show that I was unpredictable. I didn't look up to see Maithali's reaction.*

When others asked me about my reason for dropping out of college, I rolled my eyes as if I were in on a joke with them and said, 'Oh, you know, fathers.' I changed my answer depending on the recipient. I kept my reasons vague. I was moving to a different college, I had other commitments, I had a job offer, I was off to Spain. That last month in college, I pretended to complain along with the girls about my period, clutched my stomach like I had cramps. I asked for extra sanitary napkins. I stayed away from him.

In the last week before the wedding, I went to college to say goodbye to everyone. I hugged them even though I despise hugging people, and I promised to keep in touch and send them postcards, knowing fully well I wouldn't.

It was a small wedding, much smaller than my sister's, done so hurriedly that I hardly remember what it entailed. We walked around the fire, made a quick round of the mandir where I avoided looking into god's eyes. I avoided looking at my father too, because that would only remind me of my mother. I also avoided looking at my sister for most of the ceremony, but for the few seconds I did, I watched her so intensely that suddenly all her features went out of focus, and all I could see was one eye, a thread of eyebrow that looked vaguely like my mother's, a chin—all pieces of a puzzle that I recognised but couldn't tell where they fit. When I blinked, her features turned into a face, and I looked away. At some point, my stomach cramped, and I let out an involuntary yelp. My husband looked at me with concern, but I stared at my toe and blamed a loose nail on the floorboard of the mandap. I pretended to listen intently to the chants being recited by the pandit, and I could still feel his gaze on me as I took the thali in my hand and stared deep into the fire.

Later, when we shifted to his place, I looked around, marvelling at the size of the house. I was amazed at the way he had arranged his music tapes, alphabetically, the way it made sense, not by whim, colour or size like some others did. I was touched by the fact that he remembered that I felt cold at night; he had bought a thick blanket just for me. I felt safe.

My cravings were kicking in by then, and I could no longer hide them. We had had sex a couple of times at least, and while, at first, it had been awkward, even a little painful, we both found a rhythm that worked for us. I kept the lower half of my clothes on, insisted we do it in the dark. Afterwards, my husband would be lost, sometimes dazed. I'd have to call his name out loud, one, two, three times, till he responded; then he'd lean over to give me a quick kiss. Often, I couldn't shake off the burning suspicion that I wasn't the only one hiding a secret. But it was probably my own guilt talking.

My stomach was starting to stretch against the clothes I wore, and I felt myself reaching to support it subconsciously even while doing the least strenuous of tasks—picking up the clothes we had thrown on the bathroom floor, mashing together ginger and garlic to make bharta, running to answer the afternoon bell. One day, a month or so after the wedding, I felt that I would explode with either pee, anger or the baby right there and then. I sat him down on the sofa and told him that we were pregnant.

My husband was so delighted, I almost felt guilty. He hugged me tight and let me know that it was okay—that his parents too had had him after the first month of their marriage. 'In fact,' he let out a conspiratorial laugh, 'I think they had me before they got married, but they would have slapped me if I ever told them that.' I laughed along at the blasphemous idea and then went to the bathroom to puke.

That first pregnancy was a nightmare. Ashu and I were doomed from the start. I never wanted him, I had not invited him, I had not expected him, and it was as if he could tell. He made me throw up every morning, made me lurch in corridors unexpectedly. He didn't let me sit for a second in peace. If I wasn't physically ill, I was just uncomfortable, either from guilt or from a strange feeling in my belly that never settled, like dust after a storm. It just kept whirling and whirling and whirling.

I thought it would be better after Ashu was born, but I was wrong. Now I could feel the object of my guilt outside of me, and it took up so much more space than I could have imagined. How did my mother do this? How did she do this not once, but twice?

This one time, when my husband was away on a business trip, I tried to pick Ashu up after he had been crying all night. But I couldn't, he was too heavy. He weighed like a pile of bricks. I panicked, my breath tightened. I couldn't tell what was going on. I grabbed the phone and looked for the number of the hotel my husband was staying at. I couldn't find it, and I grew furious at him. He was cheating on me. He was fucking another woman. He had left me alone to deal with this mess.

But this wasn't his mess, I remembered. It was mine.

Finally, I found the name and number of the hotel. I gave him a call. He picked up, alert but curt, as though he were in the middle of a meeting. 'Are you okay? Is the baby okay?'

'I can't pick him up.'

'What?'

I repeated myself, louder now, anxious that I was already sounding like a crazy, emotional wife—the kind that husbands are always warned about. 'He's too heavy. This is not how much a normal child weighs. He keeps crying. He's too heavy.' I kept going on with the list of things that were wrong with Ashu. 'We have to get him checked. This is not normal.'

My husband stayed silent. I had to check that the telephone cord was still connected. Finally, he answered, 'I'm coming back home tomorrow.'

I put the phone down in relief. Throughout the phone call, Ashu had become curiously quiet. He was pulling himself up now, holding the bars of the cot. His tears had dried up and he looked up at me like a monster, eyes wide, the first signs of baby teeth showing like fangs from the corners of his mouth. I switched off the light and went back to bed.

The next day when my husband returned, the house was a mess. I had been lying in bed the whole day, getting up only to fetch water or feed Ashu. My husband kept his suitcase near the door, walked towards me. For a moment I felt that he had had enough. He looked at me so piercingly that I started to doubt my own proclamations the previous night. What had I said to him? Had I said that Ashu wasn't normal? Did I say anything more?

I felt something like shame. But he just bent over, enveloped me in a hug and said, 'You've done a lot. Now sleep.' He put pillows behind my back, helped me lie down, lowering me by my neck as though I were the baby. As though my body couldn't take the weight of my head. As though my head would fall off, my neck snapping in two.

I slowly drifted to sleep, and I saw my husband in a haze. He was walking towards the cot and lifting Ashu easily like he were as light as a cloud. He began tossing him up in the air, Ashu's gurgles flooding the room. Then it all went dark.

ASHU

With a few days left for school to begin, Ashu and Rahul were beginning to run out of places to visit. Rahul's home was not an option. He had a huge family and it was expanding at the seams. Rahul's father always complained about his wife's bad habit of extending an invite to anyone even remotely related to them, and now each room in their house was accommodating at least four people, if not five. As for Ashu, his home seemed more cramped than ever with Coach and Ma and Mira's holiday homework—elaborate contraptions of chart paper and glue.

It wasn't all bad though. A few months ago, a ball Ashu and Rahul had been playing with disappeared into the blue sky, and instead of getting trapped in the thick branches of the tree in front of Ashu's house, had fallen into the building's terrace. The boys had climbed up a flight of stairs and given the rough off-white door a few shoves before it fell open. After that, they spent most of the evenings there.

Ashu hadn't told Mira about their new spot, and he felt guilty when he lied to her face about running errands and snuck out to the terrace instead. However, once he climbed those steps, out of breath and completely shattered on account of his own lack of physical fitness, and found Rahul there, his back resting against the parapet, one hand in his pocket, the other holding a bottle of water, suddenly Ashu's desire to reveal his whereabouts to Mira, even think about her, faded to a distant hum at the back of his mind. Rahul would then unlock the water bottle from his lips and offer it to Ashu.

Ashu would think about Mira again only after Rahul left and Ashu dusted the white chalk off his pants. Sometimes, upon going back home, he'd see his little sister sitting with Ma on the sofa. Her saliva would dribble onto Ma's shoulder as they bent over a book, and their hair would merge into each other's so thickly, Ashu wouldn't be able to tell where Ma ended and Mira began. For a moment, Ashu would be tempted to turn around and go up to the terrace again, his guilt disappearing as quickly as it came.

But all of this would be afterwards.

Before the sun was out, Ashu and Rahul would try slinking up to the stairs sneakily, where the terrace would be alive with the sound of newly-born crows and the flutter of wet clothes that were hung to dry. Ashu and Rahul would sit with their backs against the water pump, and every so often, a rote, mechanical roar would shudder them out of their conversation. It was peaceful, a place of rest after a whole day of shuffling against sweaty and panicked girls and boys at school.

Sometimes, they'd look down at the world below and see the tops of trees, bright orange and pink and bursting with green. Down on the road, they'd see men in skull caps gathered at the chai shop, and women in salwar suits and jeans walking back from the market, their shopping bags swinging like pigtails. Near the gutter, they'd watch on as stray dogs stretched indolently, their ribs on display.

When others came to the terrace, they were often startled to see these two boys playing football, cackling so loudly it seemed like demons had taken over them. Days turned into evenings sometimes, and in the dark, Ashu and Rahul appeared taller than they really were, their shadows extended like scarecrows, well beyond their bodies. Ashu liked seeing himself like that, taller than the world and wider than a set of bricks. He'd stand there for a second, even two, and find his friend's hands waving in front of his face, and he'd laugh at being absent-minded.

Sometimes, they were told off by aunties who wanted to do their yoga there in peace. They called them rascals, and one time, even chased the boys off, wildly waving sticks used to keep stray dogs away. Ashu felt that his stomach would split at the seams and explode from how joyful he felt even when he was scared, as they ran down the stairs and out of the building, three steps at a time.

The terrace was where Ashu and Rahul found a marble on the floor, green and translucent, glowing with a twisted string inside. They had absentmindedly thrown it at a resting crow nearby. They hadn't expected it to hit, but when the bird went plummeting down to the floor, a poof of black feathers rising up to the sky, they instantly felt a stab of guilt, so revolting that both didn't look at each other for the next few days, didn't talk about it either. Maybe that's why their friendship worked, Ashu thought. They knew exactly what not to say to each other. What not to bring up again.

Once, Rahul had come to the terrace late, and Ashu had waited there for so long he had begun to wonder if he would ever arrive at all. When Rahul finally did, he looked tired and had shadows, dark and haunting, under his eyes. Ashu could tell from the way Rahul kept his face to the other side, never once turning towards Ashu, that he didn't want to be asked. Ashu felt a violent urge to protect Rahul. He twisted his fingers together and wondered why Rahul's father had raised his hands on Rahul again. Ashu didn't want to push his friend away by asking anything, however. So, he settled into the quiet of the evening, while another icicle grew.

But it was June now, when even the mosquitoes that were the eternal markers of summer quietly disappeared back into the puddles they had come from to cool themselves in the heat. The bright flowers on the trees outside Ashu and Mira's room had gone from a pleasant orange to a violent red and were starting to turn crisp and fall off the branches. It was the time when blankets were unnecessary things that fell to the floor when Ashu stretched his limbs while sleeping. The taps in the house gushed out water so hot that if he left his hand under a running stream, he felt his skin burn. Even the small mist fan couldn't rescue them from the scorching heat, and Ashu would stand near the cooler, breathing in wet spray, the smell of which lingered in his nose all day. The sun was so strong that if he looked into it directly, Ashu was sure he would lose his eyesight and wake up the next morning unable to see a thing.

'Look,' he raised his hand up now against the harsh sun. The boys were walking towards the terrace for the first time since Rahul had returned from his Nani's. Ashu hadn't been there the entire summer. He had often contemplated escaping to the rooftop with Avni but had decided against it. Somehow he didn't want to share it—this space that had become private to him and Rahul—with her.

'I look like a seal,' Ashu continued, still staring at his hairless arm.

Rahul steered Ashu's arm towards his own and kept the two side by side.

Ashu groaned. 'Okay, now that makes me feel even worse.'

'You should be glad you don't look like a bear. My father jokes that I'm growing up "too fast for my own good".' Rahul gave a hollow grin.

'Does he know—'

'About the bottles? Nah. The man wouldn't know his left hand from his right if my mom didn't hold him up straight.'

If Ashu thought that Ma was scary, Rahul's father made things at Ashu's home seem like a breeze in comparison. He didn't know the extent of Rahul's troubles, because despite his gregariousness and openness at school, Rahul was an intensely private person. Still, Ashu liked to believe that of all the friends Rahul had, Ashu was the one he confided in the most.

'Good,' Ashu laughed. 'You're really brave though. I could never imagine having the guts to do that.' He had scarcely had more than a sip of the alcohol himself that night before the summer vacation, but it had done the trick. The others had left the bottles at Rahul's. Later, it had been Ashu and Rahul who remembered to dilute the nearly empty miniatures with water and put them back in the places where they belonged. Ashu had been proud when he thought of carefully positioning the bottles around the dust patterns so they wouldn't give themselves away.

Later, though, it had all seemed to him like a very bad idea.

It had been Ishan's suggestion to drink at Rahul's in the first place. Ashu, for one, had never understood why Rahul was friends with Ishan. The boy was obnoxious and rich and mean to just about everyone. He made teachers cry on a daily basis. He was also the reason half the boys in the class were now drowning in hair gel, as they all liked to copy him. Except Rahul, of course, whose hair was wavy and completely gel-free. Whenever Ashu asked why he tolerated Ishan, Rahul only mumbled that Ishan wasn't as bad as he appeared. 'He's a decent guy,' Rahul said. But if Ishan was decent—Ashu thought when he once watched him spit on a younger boy's face for knocking over his tiffin—the standards were truly low.

Whatever the reason for their friendship, Ashu supposed that he should be grateful. Because of Ishan's strange association with Rahul, Ishan, who picked on almost all the boys in the class, didn't pick on Ashu.

They had reached the top of the staircase now. Ashu lingered behind Rahul's tall body. Rahul had suddenly stopped right before the door. Squeezing himself on the same step as Rahul, Ashu saw why.

'It's shut,' he said, stating the obvious.

'Damn it.' Rahul was toying with a cigarette in his hand, and he was obviously really looking forward to smoking it on the terrace. The door seemed to have been locked shut. A board said: 'Due to the increased use of the terrace for illicit activities, the committee has decided it will be shut until further inspection. Do not trespass or you will face consequences.'

Ashu was sure it was the aunty who had once nearly caught them smoking who was responsible for this.

'What should we do now?' Rahul looked at him. He really didn't want to go home today, Ashu could tell. 'Maybe I should punch this open,' he suggested.

Ashu knew that Rahul was strong, and if he wanted to, he probably could plough the door down. He had once heard a rumour that Rahul had punched someone on the bus because they had called Rahul names. Later, Rahul's face turned red when Ashu questioned him about it and he refused to tell him why.

'I should just tear this down,' Rahul said. 'I can do it.'

'Wait—' Ashu tried to stop him.

'I'm serious, Ash. Wherever we go, adults stop us and put us away like we're—' He scratched his head, looking for a word. '—like we're a bunch of infesting rodents.'

Ashu stifled his laughter. 'But—'

Rahul seemed to get into position to break the door open. But before Rahul could get them both into trouble, Ashu inched forward and turned towards his friend, resting both his hands on his shoulder.

'Rahul, wait. There's a place we can go.'

* * *

The pool was open and wide and large and blue, so blue it almost made Ashu's eyes hurt. He took a deep breath and inhaled the smell of shampoo, of rancid chlorine, stale floating bits of grass and dust. Rahul had already jumped into the shallow end. His tall body looked out of place there. Despite the rush of the new plan quickly wearing off—and a little nervousness settling in—Ashu couldn't help but laugh.

In the distance, people were bobbing in and out of water like moving dots. There was an older man, too, but he wasn't Coach, Ashu confirmed with a relief. The man was resting by the side of the pool and often turned around to the gutter at the side and coughed with a large, ugly noise. Ashu noticed that every person over the age of fifty coughed like that. Like they wanted attention.

'You look like a giant,' Ashu called out, and Rahul pulled a face and disappeared under the water. A few seconds later, when he emerged, he jumped up with a splash. 'Now?' he laughed. He had created a large wave and drenched Ashu with it. Nothing, Ashu observed as he looked at himself, was dry. Suddenly conscious of the way his shorts clung to his thighs, Ashu quickly jumped into the water too. He stood there, put his arms across his chest and said, 'What about me?' He bent his knees for an extra push and swivelled. 'Do I look tall?'

Behind Ashu, the sun was high, painting a golden ring around him. He felt a sparkle in his eyes, and even though he had asked the question carelessly, his body shivered ever so slightly as he stood on his toes, waiting for an answer. Most things Ashu said—like most things anyone said—were coated by a glossy film. They were neat, buffed to hide the edges of his personality. 'Do I look tall?' he said, but really, he wanted to know if he looked big, if he looked strong, if Rahul thought that Ashu could take on anyone and anything he wanted to, despite what everybody else said about him.

As though he could sense that, Rahul stopped laughing. He came closer to Ashu, gazed at him and held his friend's lean shoulders steady. He let a deep breath out and said, 'You look like the whole world.'

You know, when you're with someone you love, having a meal, maybe laughing, and you ask yourself just for a second: what would happen if I began to scream?

Or when you're walking behind a bald man on the road and are overcome by an urge to slap his shiny head?

That's how I felt those days. Seized in the most innocent of moments by an almost violent impulse. Taken over by an inexplicable desire to tell my husband the truth about our marriage. These instants came often and urgently. When we were drinking a cup of tea, when he looked calm after a hard day of work, when I saw him play with Ashu and I felt deep, resentful anger bubbling in my stomach, and it took everything out of me not to shout, 'He's not yours!'

I wondered what my husband would do if I told him the truth. Would he look at me strangely, then submit me promptly to a mental institution? Would he join me in my temporary insanity? Would he recoil and throw Ashu and me out of the house? Or would he gently, in his own way, tell me that he already knew and that he knew me to the bones? That nothing I ever did would shock him or surprise him in any way, not enough to make him want to leave me, and the two of us would fall further and further in love?

As I slowly settled into the marriage, these feelings simmered down. I was still aware of the lie, but I no longer felt tempted to say it out loud. I was happy hiding the secret deep inside me, and there were times when I even let myself forget. However, it was only when I got pregnant the second time that the impulse completely stopped.

Four years had passed quickly since the first pregnancy, and this one was the exact opposite of the first. It was joyous and playful. The two of us planned this as meticulously as he organised his music collection. We made a chart colour-coding the days I was most fertile. I laughed at that word a lot after we came back from the gynaecologist. Fertile. 'Like I'm a fucking field of wheat.'

We had sex on the kitchen counter, we had sex on the living room floor. We had sex when Ashu was sleeping, we had sex when he wasn't. All the aunties with the knowing smiles and bulging bellies always said that married people hardly had sex after the first year, and I wanted to laugh at them, say to the world, 'You thought I wouldn't be happy. Look at me now. Look at us.'

The day that Mira was born, my husband called all the numbers he remembered by heart and then took out an address book from the bedside bottom drawer. He went through every single contact on the list and said, 'I've just had a baby girl! I'm a father to a baby girl!' It became an anecdote we loved to repeat at dinner parties later—that the address book wasn't even ours. It was probably left behind by an old tenant. The people were so decent, they didn't have the heart to tell the happy stranger the truth. So they simply congratulated him and hung up the phone.

The delivery was smooth, too. Mira, she slid out of my vagina like butter. The minute she plopped out, she let out a gurgle. And although I had hated the gurgle of babies—on flights, in buses, at bookstores—my heart took a little leap when I heard hers. I just knew it was going to be easier this time around. But it's a rather well-known rule in life that the minute you want to wave your fortune about and tell the world how happy you are, it's all taken away. Maybe it's how the universe restores balance. A sort of cosmic punishment for daring to show off. Maybe that's why my mother had always feared god.

One night, I was up at 1 a.m., breastfeeding Mira. By this time, I had become quite accustomed to the painful process of giving milk and didn't resist when she cried out for more. Ashu was sleeping in the room next to us; he was now nearly five, and although he was heavy like a pile of bones, my husband would pick him up and carry him around. He agreed only reluctantly, and at my insistence, that it was time that Ashu began sleeping in his own room. But he would—and I noticed—under the pretext of going to the bathroom, check on Ashu at night and come back to me without saying a word.

I was engrossed in feeding Mira that night, and it was only when my husband switched on the bedside light that I realised I was actually humming out loud, loud enough to wake him up. I grinned sheepishly at him and whispered sorry. He pretended to be annoyed. He pecked at my chin like he was a chicken and then at my free breast. One thing led to another, as things do, and we transferred Mira to the cot. Although my husband was evidently sleepy, we both grabbed each other fervently, my hands running down his legs, him toying with my top. That's when the doorbell started ringing.

It was a tiny ring at first, and the two of us were too busy to care. No one rang our bell that late at night. We ignored it all for a couple of minutes when someone started beating the door. It began small like a heartbeat that you feel faintly when you rest your head on someone's chest. Then it started rising in crescendo, a large drum beating louder and louder. We looked at each other with alarm. Who could be at the door at this hour? I leapt out of bed to check on the baby, and my husband sprang out of the room to see that Ashu was still asleep.

Mira was fine, so I adjusted my top, threw on a robe to open the door, when my husband stopped me and walked ahead. The door swung open and I looked at the visitor.

It was Ashu's father. And he was drunk.

I felt as though the soles of my feet had suddenly sprouted roots. I couldn't move, I could hardly talk, I couldn't breathe. My husband looked puzzled; he didn't know who it was. 'Sir, I think you have the wrong house,' he said in a loud voice and tried to shut the door, but I rooted out my feet and walked ahead to stop him.

'What—what are you doing here?' I spluttered at the figure at the door.

Nikhil was standing outside our house, the house I shared with my husband.

'How could you not tell me?' he slurred. He was wasted, I could tell by the way he swung his arms when he spoke, the way his full hair was dishevelled; his skin looked leathery and pale. I felt that he had aged at least fifty years since I had last slipped into the car with him.

I blinked.

My own husband, I noticed, was standing away from me now. He seemed to be trying to gauge how I knew this drunk man, who he was to me. I tried to catch my husband's attention, tell him that I had no idea what was happening, ask him to take this detestable man away, but he wasn't locking eyes with me anymore.

'I ran into Maithali—she said you got married.' Nikhil continued his monologue, his breath heavy with alcohol. 'She even told me you have two fucking children now,' he spat. 'Two!'

His profanity sprung me into action. I pushed him away outside the threshold of the house. I wanted to usher him away from my husband before things went past the point of no return. 'Wait outside,' I said sternly to Nikhil. I framed it as an order, but I knew I was pleading.

While he waited at the other side of the door, I went back to my husband. He was standing still with an odd expression on his face. Was it anger? I didn't have time to judge. I quickly apologised to him, holding him by his shoulder and telling him, 'It's just an old friend. He's drunk. He's going through a divorce. I'll see him out.'

My husband shifted his weight from one foot to the next. 'This is ridiculous,' he said quietly.

'I know. I know it is. I'll tell him off. Make sure it doesn't happen again. You go check on the children.'

When he didn't move, again I said. 'Sweetie, I'm serious. The children are alone. Go, go.'

When he finally left, I slammed the door behind him shut, neatly slicing the air between Ashu's father and my family into two.

Outside, it was cold. I could feel my ears grow red, and in the relative silence of the night, my heart beat loud. In the two minutes I had left him alone, Nikhil had collapsed. He was wobbling near the front of the door. His back was hunched over, and he was puking near the plant from which I picked curry leaves every morning. He looked pathetic and slimy, like a slug left over after the rain. I couldn't believe I was ever attracted to him.

When he was done, I grabbed his wrist with more power than I realised I had. I whispered furiously, 'Just what do you think you're doing here?'

He lunged towards me. 'I heard—you've got kids. Why didn't you tell me?'

I shrugged him off. He smelt so strongly of the cheap whisky we all used to drink in college. I wanted to get away. 'It's none of your business.'

'But—' It was evident from his expression that he was trying to calculate something, and it showed on his face. 'How old is he? Your oldest one?'

I lied.

'Are you sure? Maithali told me you had him in the middle of—wait, is that why you left?'

'Would I not remember when my own son was born, Nikhil?' I snapped. 'Really, you're being ridiculous. And you cannot ever enter my house like this at night and startle my family.'

He made a face. Now he looked like a sorrowful slug.

'I'm sorry. But you weren't picking up my calls. You haven't spoken to me in a while.'

It was true. I hadn't. 'That doesn't mean—' I waited while he bent over to throw up some more. I changed tack. 'Just—don't ever contact me again.'

When he got up, there was something dribbling down his neck. For a moment, I felt tempted to wipe it off the way I'd wipe Mira's chin most days.

Then, I felt a shadow over my shoulder. I glanced behind me. My husband was looking through the window. I gestured at him that it would only take a second more, and I stepped further away from the man.

'But what about us?' he continued. He sounded like a child now. Wailing, unloved.

I stayed quiet. I had met Nikhil a few months after Ashu was born. We had coffee outside. He sat down and complained about academics and worried if he should focus on his job search or study for his MBA entrance exams. He asked me no questions, spoke about himself the entire time. I was so angry with him that I thought of telling him about Ashu and making him pay. But I ended up saying nothing. For, I sensed that if I said it out loud, I'd give the truth power. As he talked, he reached for my hand underneath the oblong table, and later, in his car, tried to kiss me as he dropped me home. I came back from the meeting with a feeling of slime on my body that I couldn't wash off for days.

'You must be unhappy,' he said once he had puked. 'Be with me.'

'No,' I said firmly. There were no instincts to fight this time. 'That was a mistake.'

'But—'

'There's nothing for you here. Go.'

As he walked away, I was pulled by an urge to pick up a rock and throw it at his head. I could see it split his head and the blood pooling around him, rendering him still and unable to cause harm to anyone. No one would get to know, I thought. No one would care. But I stopped myself. For a moment, the man looked just like Ashu. Vague, naïve. Unsure of the physics of his body as he sat in the car.

He drove away.

I really did want to kill him. But I missed my chance.

* * *

After that, I was wary of everything around me. I unplugged the landline from the cord, I didn't step out. I switched the TV on mindlessly only to realise it later. I stopped reading. I kept one eye open when a tree branch scraped too loudly against our window, felt alarmed by a hollow knock at the door. I kept Mira by my side most times. I even patrolled Ashu's room often to make sure that he was still in there. Because of this, I felt tired all the time. Even Ashu noticed it. 'My Ma loves sleeping,' he declared at playschool and told me about it proudly later. I winced.

Like a child, I cried if left alone in a dark room. I never used to be afraid of the darkness earlier. I had always been a somewhat brazen child. It used to be hard to perturb me. I would find ghost stories fascinating and would watch the horror shows that aired on TV at night with mild curiosity, not knowing why my sister shuddered and my mother pulled her sari pallu close to her face. She used to be terrified, my mother. She thought that I'd just wander off somewhere into the distance some day and not return. 'She doesn't know what it is to be afraid,' I heard her tell my father once when I refused to turn off the television. 'Go on. Tell her to stop.'

My sister had been the first one who had warned me when we were younger. The lights had gone out one day and she had been sitting unusually quietly in the dark. I asked her what was wrong, and she said that she was afraid of what was out there. Ghosts and spirits didn't exist, I said, to reassure her, but she looked annoyed, even surprised that I didn't believe her. 'Look'—she put her arm around my neck and pointed at something in the air—'they're here right now.' She whispered, her breath warm on my neck. 'Can't you see?'

My husband did everything to distract me. He made plans to go out with friends, asked me join a book club. Sometimes, Ashu sensed my mood, climbed over me and tried to pull faces, but I pushed him away.

When nothing worked, my husband changed tack. He interrogated me about what was wrong, asked if it had anything to do with my old friend coming by the other night. I denied everything.

It was as though someone had poured acid over the impulse I once harboured to tell him the truth about Ashu. Nikhil's visit made me hold on to the secret even more tightly. I was terrified that my husband would find out.

Most of the time, I realise now, I wasn't even sad. I just felt empty. Like a house that had been broken into in the middle of the night, and now nothing was left to take.

I thought about my mother a lot those days. I dreamt about her vividly, could touch her soft, sagging skin in my sleep only to wake up and realise that I had been grabbing wisps of air. In those moments, I almost picked up the phone to call my sister, but then I remembered how she'd distanced herself from me the moment she got married and the disappointed tone of her voice when I did get in touch. Some days, I thought I could feel my mother's hand on my scalp, stroking it round and round in circles at the spot which always flaked. One day, I could smell camphor in the air. I was convinced that the maid had bought some and stored it in the house. I turned the house upside down; I looked through boxes of pills, then boxes of silver, as though the burning white thing would be hiding inconspicuously among mirrored rings and anklets. I even looked through my husband's shirts, one by one, tossing them in the air in an almost decadent, Gatsby-esque manner, until I was sitting among a heap of clothes when he came home from work. He convinced me that neither the maid nor he had bought any camphor, that they knew that I was allergic to it and he would never allow it to enter the house. Nevertheless, I fired the maid. I couldn't bear to have her look at me with either pity or curiosity. I didn't know which was worse.

Ashu cried a lot that day because the maid took care of him the most. For days afterwards, he wailed. He called her name in his sleep, he woke up from naps looking lost. He looked for her under the bed, below tables.

He even opened my mouth one day and searched inside it as though I were a monster who had swallowed his maid and then kept her hidden between the teeth to chew up slowly. I looked at my husband in exasperation. Should we hire her again? He shook his head. What was done was done. Ashu continued with this for a few days more, crying and searching alternately. Soon after, like children do, he forgot.

MIRA

Every day is so slow and hot, it feels like we are sitting inside the sun. I run around Ashu to try and get his attention, but he always acts busy like he has many meetings and has to go to office—as though he's a Mr Busyman or something. But really, he just goes out with Rahul for hours and comes back smelling like feet.

Coach comes over some days, but less than before. When he does visit, I sit on the sofa and watch him and Ma chat and chat away. They talk about grown-up things like how much sugar is alright to have and why the rain is late this time, and all the while they're holding hands tight and sweaty. I stare at the floor and my heart goes thump-thump so loud like the clock in the living room that I wonder how Ma can't hear it. When Ashu's also there, he rolls his eyes at Coach and talks to me. But sometimes, like when Ma goes to get her purse or goes to make some tea, it's just Coach and me, like that day at my party, except this time, we don't talk to each other. We don't say a single word, not a hi, not a hello, how are you, not an anything at all.

One night, I have a dream. I'm watching TV in our living room. Only the TV is bigger, and all the shows and ads, even the cartoons inside it, are appearing in black-and-white. I am sitting on the sofa alone because Ma's in her room and Ashu's stepped out for a walk. I hold on tight to the remote because any minute Ashu will come and say Silly goose, it's time for the grown-ups to watch TV! And he'll snatch the remote from me.

All of a sudden, the lights go out, and everything stops working, even the TV. It's so dark in the room that I can't even see my fingers or my toes and I have to touch them to check that they are still there on my body. Then a sound starts playing from the TV. It's a small voice, and I go closer to listen to it. Let me see the butterfly, baby, it says softly through the TV. I say nothing. I hear: Do you want your Ma to be lonely? Only this time, I want to shout *Yes, let her*! but my mouth says no, a big round no, just like last time, only bigger and louder. And Coach starts to laugh.

Ashu is still snoring when my eyes open, and my T-shirt is sweaty all the way through. I blink my eyes, looking at our cupboard which is right in front of me. The glow-in-the-dark T-shirt is there at the back, crumpled behind my Going Out clothes and Staying In clothes. I imagine the doors slowly opening on their own, and I blink so hard I start to see little swirls inside my eyes. I can almost see little butterflies, pink and blue in colour. They are flying out of the cupboard, they are flying out of the window. They are even flying out of our home forever.

SINK

ASHU

'You smell funny.'

Mira and Ashu were plopped on the bed, and Ashu was observing his legs as he rested them against the wall. Veins like thin green caterpillars ran down his ankles. He had seen such lines on Ma before. In places least expected—underneath her feet, at the back of her neck, on the underside of her arms. He must have gotten it from her.

Mira repeated herself, and Ashu brought himself back to the moment. His sister was hanging upside down from his bed, and he was on hers. She looked like a bat, Ashu idly observed.

'*You* smell funny,' he said mindlessly. He was still thinking about how unexpectedly good the day had turned out. Mira must have smelt the water on him, the stickiness of the club, the auto ride, the oily fat of French fries that they had wanted to eat but didn't have enough money for. Oddly, today he didn't feel guilty.

It was risky to go to the club. Rahul *had* checked with Ashu if Coach would be there and rat them out to Ma. In a role reversal, Ashu was the one who bravely said *nah*, he won't be there. It was true. Coach only took classes in the mornings those days. Ashu knew this because Coach spoke about it whenever he was at their house, his legs spread wide on the sofa, his arms resting on his thighs and his loud mouth telling stories about the time he first swam in a small stream in his village and afterwards ate a full fish from it with bones and everything. The stories were mildly fascinating, but only if you knew they were going to end.

Unlike Mira, Ashu loved being at the club. There were so many chatty people who walked around the place that he felt that he didn't have to talk at all. Everyone moved with an air of urgency and Ashu felt like a chameleon who could blend in, become anyone, and he liked that. He did.

Mira threw a cushion at him now, not daring to target his face, and it landed softly on his stomach. Ashu grabbed it, turned over and fell into deep, sweet sleep.

* * *

The June afternoons got hotter and hotter, and the boys continued to go to the club. Sometimes, they snuck in there a few minutes after Ma had slipped into her afternoon nap. It made Ashu's stomach tingle with excitement, the ways in which he could lie now. It surprised him how easily, especially when it came to making plans to swim with Rahul, he could set the expression on his face to fool Ma. *I'm going to Rahul's to do homework. We're just stepping out for a walk. We are*—Well, to be honest, he could have said anything or nothing. Ma didn't seem to care.

In the water, Ashu felt free. He had learnt how to swim from Rahul over the last few weeks. Ashu preferred to keep his head above the surface most of the time, but he was a powerful swimmer. Even though it looked like Rahul would be the better one, Ashu's small frame afforded him an agility in the water that let him cut through it easily, moving much faster than he ever did on land.

One evening, there was a dust storm right as they reached the club. It was the kind of storm that came unexpectedly in the middle of summer, strong winds and gusts of rain breaking branches and shifting cars, turning everything over. The sky had become dull and grey, and Rahul and Ashu changed their minds as soon as they reached the pool. The wind was bellowing in their ears.

'This is terrible.' Rahul winced as bits of grit entered his eye. He covered them with his hands and stumbled on the concrete. 'Ashu!' he said when he couldn't find his path. Ashu laughed and guided his friend back towards the entrance. 'Let's get out of here,' he said.

They were just about to leave when Ashu saw Coach from the corner of his eye. He was holding a boy by his hand and helping him to the changing room. Ashu ducked to avoid him, but thought it strange to see Coach there at that time of the day. As Rahul pulled his arm, Ashu brushed the thought aside.

* * *

On the last Saturday before summer vacation ended, Rahul came to Ashu's house almost an hour later than he should have. Ashu opened the door as soon as it rang. Standing there was Rahul, and his eyes looked red.

'What's wrong?' Ashu choked on the question when he noticed that it wasn't just a red eye, there was blood. Had Rahul gotten into trouble at home again?

Ashu stepped aside to let Rahul enter.

'I thought I wouldn't come—' Rahul mumbled and turned his face slightly away. 'I kind of hit a rock on the road and started, er, bleeding.'

Ashu looked Rahul in the eye. They both knew the story wasn't true, but they had learnt to navigate the contours of their friendship this way. He stayed silent and went to the kitchen.

Rahul sat on the marble floor outside the kitchen, waiting. 'Where's your mom?' he called out.

Ashu didn't respond but came back with some ice cubes wrapped in a thin towel and slid onto the floor next to him.

'Out with Mira,' he shrugged. 'She'll be back soon though—so let's get the blood cleaned up fast.'

Rahul sat patiently, and Ashu got to his knees. He began to gently wipe Rahul's eyes with the towel and winced as he imagined how much it must be hurting. Ashu was not feeling his best either. Ma had been downcast for a couple of days, and no one had been able to make her feel better. Mrs Shome had tried, but Ma stayed in bed even when she visited, the full cups of tea before her accumulating dust. When Ashu went to check on her in the evening, he saw Ma lying on her bed like a statue he'd once seen at a museum, lifeless and still.

Ma became like this often. A paler version of herself. Under blankets in a dark room. She stayed in bed all day. She made Mira and Ashu field calls from work and make excuses on her behalf. 'Tell them I'm down with the flu,' she hissed in her nightie from behind the frame of her door. She only took Coach's calls. Sometimes, even though Ashu felt rather mean considering it, he maybe even preferred Ma this way. When she was like this, she had none of her usual energy to snap at things, to make tiny but biting comments about the way Ashu sat while watching TV, with his legs crossed, one on top of the other.

Still, Ashu hesitated at the threshold of her door when he entered to give her yet another cup of tea. Entering Ma's room rarely ended well for him, even under the best of circumstances. He often returned bruised in places he didn't know it was possible to be hurt in (his heart, his head, the small part of his chest) from things he didn't know it was possible to be hurt about (how he raised his eyebrows, how he always woke up late, how long he let his toenails grow, the way he breathed). With Ma, Ashu never felt brave enough, boy enough.

Ashu was unlike Ma in most ways. He hadn't gotten her nose; her love of reading had skipped him and gone straight to Mira; he didn't understand most things she said. He wondered: of all the things he could inherit from Ma, would it be her sadness? Often, he wanted to sit Ma down and ask her things. He wanted to know what she had been like when she was his age. Had she ever failed at a subject at school? Had she fallen in love? Did she have vivid dreams about strangers the way he did? And had she always felt *this* way? Ma had mentioned once that she had just woken up one morning when she was older and realised that there wasn't much to be happy about. Would Ashu, too, wake up one day, feel sad and want to climb into bed and go back to sleep for a long time? Would it happen when he turned fifteen, twenty, thirty? Would it happen to Mira too?

But question words belonged to Mira, and Ashu didn't use them.

Now, as he moved the cold towel which was dripping water on to the floor, he tried not to think about any of this. The only sound was of the fridge humming.

'Done the homework?' Rahul broke the silence.

Ashu thought of the fifty pages of homework they had been assigned over the summer.

'Oh, yeah,' he said flatly. 'All.'

Rahul gave him a grin. 'Honestly, but why do they think we don't have better things to do over the summer? It's like they *want* us to be miserable,' he said.

Ashu shrugged. 'I actually don't think I had anything better to do—for the most part.'

'Really?' Rahul sat up straighter. 'I thought you had a great summer with your Mausi.' The blood above his eyebrows was starting to merge with the ice water and turn a pale pink. It reminded Ashu of the iodine tincture Ma often put in a bucket of water. When he was younger, he would sit down on the bathroom floor and watch as Ma added drops from the tiny maroon bottle into a large bucket of water, and the solution would swirl and swirl and swirl, transforming from a deep red rose to a pale pink. Then she would make Ashu fetch her a towel to soak up the excess water that would've splashed outside and shoo him out so she could dip her feet in it in peace.

'Well. I mean, I swam. A lot.' Ashu caught his friend's eye and grinned.

'Sure.'

'And I met family. Family that I didn't even know existed before this.'

'All perfectly normal things.'

Ashu's mind shot to something else. 'And, er—' he said.

Rahul sat up even straighter, if it were possible. 'And?' he probed.

'I almost kissed someone.' Ashu mumbled this sentence so quietly that he was sure Rahul had barely been able to hear him. He had been keeping the weird incident from Rahul, but it came out right then, without any notice to himself.

Rahul let out a quick short laugh. 'Kissed someone? Good for you, dude.' He said the words the same way he said most, but to Ashu, Rahul sounded like he was trying to keep a frog from leaping out of his throat.

'Who's the—girl, man?' Rahul laughed again. There was something strange about the way Rahul was talking to him. For one, they never called each other 'man' or 'dude.' It was hilarious when they heard other boys in class like Manav or Ishan do that—as though they were Americans.

Ashu laughed, but uncomfortably. There was no way he was going to tell Rahul the circumstances under which this almost-kiss had happened and with whom. Had anything noteworthy even transpired? Ashu tried to remember, but the harder he pushed himself to recall, the foggier his memory became. The only images that his brain could conjure up were the close-up of a mango bark, its jagged lines jutting out, and a line of fat, red ants marching along. And dust, a lot of dust. He shook his head and said, 'It was nothing. I was kidding.'

Rahul looked at him uncertainly, like he didn't believe him, but true to their code, he kept his silence and nodded briskly.

They continued to sit together on the floor. The fan was whirring; outside, from the corner of his eye, Ashu could see the trees moving gently, and a bee—or a wasp—he could never tell the difference—aggressively trying to enter through the window. Ashu was tempted to let it in.

'Mannn...' Rahul buried his head in his hands.

Ashu looked at him with concern and confusion. 'What? Does it hurt?'

Rahul said softly, 'I don't know.'

Ashu felt a warm, arrhythmic buzzing in his ear. He jerked his head to the side and checked, but the wasp was still outside, struggling to get past the window. The familiar feeling at the back of Ashu's knees had returned too, but this time, it was rising quickly, spreading all over his body, whooshing around his knees, up his bony thighs, closer up towards his chest like pollen travelling in the wind.

Maybe that's what pushed him to move forward, to hold Rahul's hand. He didn't know what he was doing, but it was all he could think about. They had held hands before, only briefly, while crossing the road and trying to pull the other along, or while passing a cigarette. But that was nothing. This was different.

Rahul unburied his head and looked up at him. Ashu couldn't tell what Rahul was thinking. The bravery that Ashu had felt in the moment's heat drained from him like blood, and he snatched his hand back, depositing it in his pocket, next to his own body, where it had always belonged. 'Sorry,' Ashu mumbled. 'I—I didn't mean to.'

But Rahul wasn't upset. He seemed, if Ashu was correct, to be shifting closer to him.

Ashu placed the soaked towel onto the floor and waited for him to say something. He was aware of each point where their bodies were in contact. Their knees were touching now, Ashu's leaning towards Rahul, Rahul's falling back on Ashu's. He stared at the rough edge of the denim that Rahul was wearing. These were the same jeans he always wore, the same ones he'd worn even when they had rushed to the terrace the first time and found themselves under the open blue sky. The same ones he had worn before they had jumped into the pool.

It was Rahul who grabbed Ashu's hand now. And this time, he was playing with it, rubbing the skin around his thumb where it must've peeled off when Ashu bit his nails.

'Ash,' he whispered so softly that Ashu could barely hear it. 'Can I *please* just kiss you?'

Ashu knew he was gone, far gone, even before he could move closer to Rahul. Even before he could touch his hand, even before he could make sure he had heard him correctly, he knew that this was it. This, the moment he would fall in love, and something fundamental in him would alter forever. 'What?' he mouthed. He suddenly felt very aware of his own breath, how it expanded and contracted through his body, how it moved in short, sharp bursts within his chest.

The afternoon sun was coming straight into his eyes like the headlights of a car on high beam. Rahul began to move towards him. Soft, golden hair ran faintly down Rahul's arms like the lines of a country, visible now to Ashu only because he was sitting so close to him. Rahul asked Ashu the question again. This time, Ashu heard it clearly. There was no mistaking it. He nodded and closed his eyes.

Rahul's lips pressed against his lightly. They felt flaky and soft; he tasted like sweat and cloves. As they sat on the speckled floor, Ashu slowly began to press back harder. He felt something like confidence come upon him. He had never wanted anything more. He got to his knees, not caring if they would get scraped by the floor and leaned down towards Rahul, kissing him hungrily, urgently. Now, he was taller than Rahul, taller than he himself had ever been. The harsh headlights in his eyes dimmed, the sky turned orange. Something warm like clear, bright sunlight started flowing down his entire body. When they pulled apart slightly, Ashu looked at his friend and smiled. The icicles had finally begun to melt.

* * *

It was the most bearable Sunday Ashu had ever had. It fluctuated in its tempo—slowed down when he was dreaming of the day before, quickened when he realised how much homework he genuinely had left to do. While usually Ashu moped around on the last day of vacation, today he felt buoyant—like he had just been told by someone that he never had to go to school again. Nah, but now Ashu liked the idea of school, in fact, he *wanted* to go to school. Rahul and he had spent the rest of last evening holding hands, smiling without any reason at all. Ashu wanted to see Rahul again, to explore what it felt like to kiss him, to do it for minutes, even hours at a stretch. To sit next to him in class, push their chairs closer together than before, so that not only would their knees touch, but the tips of their shoes, the sides of their legs too. It didn't matter anymore, he supposed, who loved him and how much and why, when he could feel this happy.

Always, always, in Ashu's head, there had been too many

thoughts jostling around for space. He could hear them, all the time, too many of them, all at once. But right now, these thoughts—the dreams of strange oily-haired women, the sounds of ghosts knocking against doors, the awful feelings he carried within him inside cars and in places with low ceilings—simply stopped. It didn't matter. They didn't exist.

It lasted like this for a while. This space between the real and the surreal. I became comfortable in it. I even began to seek pleasure in it. Soon, the days after Nikhil's visit in the night turned into weeks, and the weeks turned into months.

Slowly, I started to get involved in life again. The cloud over my heart felt less heavy. I was no longer fearful all the time, afraid that the vile man would show up at my door. My husband was the first one to see it. 'You look happy,' he declared when he came home from work. I thought about it for a second and realised that maybe I was happy. I then noticed that I hadn't really looked at my husband properly for the past few months. He had been working a lot, and his office trips had increased. He was travelling nearly every weekend. He had started fading away. He looked thin and tired, his trousers hanging loose on him. He hadn't been eating. Suddenly missing the girth of his stomach. I decided to do something. I started cooking and spending more time in the kitchen. I made paranthas to fatten him up. I sent large tiffins his way. He began to put on weight. He blamed me, but he was only kidding.

I remember him getting all excited—worked up even—about Mira's first birthday which was fast approaching. 'Let's throw a party,' he said, and I gave him a look. 'Right, right. Well, how about we go for a holiday? Just the four of us?'

After days of convincing, he wore me down.

Mira was crawling all over the floor now. She was babbling like a brook. I never understood how mothers could follow their children around and record their every move. It was not fascinating to me to see a smaller version of a full-sized adult function at less-than-half capacity and fail to do even the most basic tasks properly. Maybe that was the golden period, before she learnt to speak and ask all the questions that she's learnt to ask since then.

Having been compelled to call my sister 'di', I did not want Mira to call Ashu 'bhaiya'. Yet Mira was obsessed with Ashu. She would crawl from her cot to his room, and even if I woke up to separate them, in the morning I'd inevitably find her in his bed, sleepy eyed and holding his arm. Ashu, too, played along. He thought they looked like twins even though they couldn't have looked less alike. He'd squish his face next to hers, nearly smothering her, and I'd have to pull him away. 'Look,' he'd say in a bubbling, syrupy voice. 'Same.'

The day before our trip, Mira had a bad tummy, and she kept throwing up. I oscillated between feeling sorry for her and sorry for myself. 'Looks like we're going to have to cancel,' I said to my husband while rubbing Mira's back half-heartedly.

His face fell, and I felt like I could do anything to get that look off his face. Ashu was lingering nearby, offering to get water or something absolutely useless for babies. My husband could see that Ashu was getting on my nerves, so he pulled him closer to look after him until I fixed Mira.

Finally, by the end of the day, Mira's stomach settled. She fell asleep, and when she woke up, she looked for me crying, as though I was lost. When she finally located me, she heaved a sigh of relief and blurted out her first word, like she had been holding on to it for months and months and couldn't take it any longer. Ma, she cried. And she hasn't stopped saying it since.

* * *

The journey was endless. We sat in a car, then a ferry, then a plane, then a cab. Through it all, the children went through varying degrees of sickness. At some point when we were halfway through the flight, Mira's ears popped and she started crying incessantly. I held her at an arm's distance, embarrassed to be the source of all the commotion. My husband and I had only managed to get separate seats—I had Mira with me; he had Ashu. Eventually a harried-looking attendant came over and offered Mira a sweet to suck on. The attendant's hair was pulled back into a tight bun. She asked me if I had given Mira any medication for the journey, and when I said no, looked disturbed that I hadn't taken this minor detail of flying with infants into account, that I didn't know the basics of motherhood. I wished to tell her to fuck off, but my husband was watching.

When we were somewhere over the ocean, my husband got up and went to the washroom. Ashu toddled off behind him into the aisle, his feet moving faster than the rest of his body. Of course he fell flat. By then my husband had already locked himself into the cubicle stall, not realizing that Ashu had been following him. The attendant ran to help Ashu up. She held him by his pinky finger and looked around to see whom he belonged to. I waved from my seat, and she started walking towards me. My husband exited the stall right then and came to hug Ashu from the back. The attendant looked up at him, surprised, and said, 'Yours?' When he nodded, she put her hand up to her mouth and looked back at me, tracing my face, then Ashu's, then his. My back began to sweat. I jumped up, grabbed Ashu and kept him sitting still for the rest of the flight.

When we finally reached Rome—Mira had been ensconced in my husband's arms for the rest of the flight—I was glad to be rid of the stale, suffocating air of the plane. It was my first time abroad. I didn't know that it would be my last. Before my mother died, my sister and I used to drop hints to our parents about wanting to travel to a foreign country. Often, our father simply buried his head into his fingers, hoping that by the time he looked up again, we would have stopped talking about the things he couldn't give us. Sometimes, when he was in a good mood, he joked about going abroad with my mother by pointing at the snow-covered Alps on the TV screen and saying, 'Kaafi beautiful, na?' or even, 'Maybe we should go there.' Then he and our mother would burst into peals of hysterical laughter, my father clutching his stomach with one hand and my mother's hand with the other.

Maybe I shouldn't have been surprised then by how taken I was with Italy. How much bluer the skies seemed, how much sweeter the crusty bread, how much more cinched the waists of the women, how much more handsome the men. I was a foolish tourist, fascinated by the cobbled streets but unable to see the dirt jammed between the stones.

On most days, we left Mira and Ashu at the place of a friend of my husband's from college. 'Go. Va, va, have fun,' he and his wife insisted with a kind of urgency we couldn't refuse and shoved us out the door. They probably aren't able to have children of their own, I told my husband later. That's why they're so desperate for ours.

We went for long, languorous meals where we ate until the buttons of our clothes stretched to reveal our stomachs. We had gnocchi bursting with cheese and oil, and pizza so soft, it folded over itself like skin. We laughed at the way the server looked at us when asked for chilli flakes to add to everything. After eating, we sprawled under the sun like cats with little to do but sneer at others. We went on long passeggiatas around the neighbourhood and ended up in alleys that were wide open at one end and progressively got slimmer at the other. No surprises about what we did there.

Over the trip, we tried to pick up the language, simple everyday words like ciao, come stai, non parliamo Italiano, non è mio figlio, mi sono persa, dov'è? but they sat funny on our tongues, strange, unpleasant. We argued, we fought, we got gelato and made up. We let the sun form pin prickles on our skin and rashes on our necks. We fought some more. I noticed that my husband had started getting tired more quickly than I did. He heaved when we climbed winding staircases in cathedrals, had to stop often to catch his breath.

On the days we took the children sightseeing with us, we were the most troubled. Mira and Ashu had triple the energy of what they had back home. They were happy one minute, cranky the next. They ate like little monsters, no amount of pizza satisfied them. It was only when we found a family-run Indian restaurant and fed them simple food—roti, dal, sabzi and achaar—that they passed out for hours afterwards in a stupor that can only be induced by food from home.

Throughout the trip, there was so much walking to do, they had to be carried. They didn't seem to understand that we were not in our country, that there were certain rules we had to abide by, things we couldn't say. Ashu, in particular, couldn't tell that here in a sea of cerulean, his skin was dark blue. That when he spoke, the sounds that came out of his mouth sounded different to those who were listening. He was oblivious to the customs of being a tourist and had a reckless arrogance in the way he went up to strangers' tables and asked them for their bread basket if they weren't eating from it. Watching him made me feel restless from within. My husband always laughed it off, like it was funny or even adorable to watch your kid stumble around the world like that. It wasn't. I decided that I would have to put a stop to it. My husband was too lenient. No. It would be my job to make sure Ashu understood the rules, learnt how to treat women, that he knew how to behave.

Mira, on the other hand, was born with a question mark etched on her face. She noticed everything. The slightest shift in shade, the smallest glance in expression. Even at home, she could sense when my husband and I were arguing in whispers or being quiet only for the sake of the children. She'd immediately start howling. In Italy, too, when we fought, she glanced at her father and me as though unable to choose the culprit of the situation. Despite the charade of trying to choose, however, she always crawled up to me in the end, cupping my face with her chubby hands, and said in her newly found words, 'Ma? Sad?' or 'Ma? Cry?' Afterwards, both Ashu and she moaned to go back to my husband's friend's place, where they had the adults' undivided attention. We obliged.

My husband and I couldn't wait to get our hands on each other. It was the crisp sheets, the vile, private feeling of knowing that others had done this here before, that there would be others after us again. But there was something different about the way he was with me in Italy. It was urgent. Less patient. We brought the strangeness of the day into bed, we took out the frustration of never fully knowing whether someone on the street was complimenting or insulting us out on each other's bodies. At night, we did it silently, moving like shadows under the sheets, crinkling them with every move, shushing one another so the kids wouldn't wake up.

We went to Florence for a day and got lost at the museum. We went to Pisa too. We contemplated going to Venice but changed our minds because I had heard it was no more attractive than the Ganga at best. My husband agreed to everything I said and scratched existing plans off the itinerary at a moment's notice. We kissed, then kissed some more. This became the honeymoon we never had. By the time Ashu had grown into a semblance of a human being who could walk and talk and do things by himself, we had already started planning for our second baby. My husband worked hard, he had been saving up for this. I cuddled up to him when I realised how much this trip must have cost. I gave him a little extra love at night, did things he was too polite to ask for.

One afternoon, the weather suddenly decided to turn on its head. It was as grey as the streets. We were sitting in a café, and my husband was making me fill the customs form for the journey back. I hesitated as always at the section where we had to fill our occupations. I wrote 'housewife' in a hurry, remembered how Maithali and the other girl whose name started with K in college looked at me when they learnt that I was getting married.

People who were cycling to work had stopped under the awnings of cafes across the street. A group of girls, pale, young, tall, were huddled together and holding their university books over their head like umbrellas. Their efforts at protecting themselves from the rain were laughable. I tried to lean closer. They seemed like they were reading novels. Maybe they were literature students. They had that haphazard, aimless look about them as they laughed and splayed their fingers over their hair.

It had been a bit of a struggle to convince my middle-class parents that I wanted to study literature. Probably these girls, too, had to convince their parents that it was a worthwhile subject. Were they studying in Italian or English? Did they want to become teachers? Perhaps they didn't even like to read, but had met a boy in high school who claimed he liked Ayn Rand.

I hadn't realised that while I was observing the street, a server had appeared beside our table and had been asking me, 'Il suo caffé? Signora? Caffé?'

Even though my husband had gestured to him to place the coffee on the table, the man insisted on getting my attention. I looked at him, accepted the cup, and took a sip. It was bitter.

'What were you thinking about?' My husband leaned in.

I shrugged. 'Just looking.'

'At those girls? Such a creep.'

I shoved his shoulder playfully. 'I was trying to see what they're reading.'

'Why don't you ask them?'

'Yes, and then I'll go ask them about their sex lives and what keeps them up at night.'

He clutched his heart in mock pain, then said more seriously, 'Do you miss it?'

I acted dumb.

He stressed, 'You know. Before. Do you wish that—things—were different?' He always treaded carefully when it came to my mother. He thought I was heartbroken after her sudden death. If only he knew that was just the beginning, there were many little deaths that took place in me after.

I held his hand and stared ahead. The sky was clearing, and the girls were now shrieking, dropping their damp books into their bags and cycling away. Before I could respond, the server had come back. He dropped small packets of sugar on to the smooth tabletop and nodded efficiently. While he was walking away, I felt something on my shoulder and I looked up. Sometimes, even today in an idle moment, I wonder if the waiter had touched my neck by accident. Or if he, like other men before him, after him, did it on purpose. Grazed his uninvited fingers along my bare shoulder for a moment too long, leaving it there tingling.

On the last night of our trip, my husband dressed up in a black tuxedo. He reminded me of a penguin. A very suave penguin, I added out loud to him from behind the bathroom door while I got ready. His face fell for a second, then he saw that I was kidding. I wore a long maroon dress, and it swept the ground as I walked. I had kohled the waterline of my eyelid so dark that it stung my eyes, and I let tears drip down for a second. He said I looked gorgeous, a compliment he knew I always loved. I liked the way he complimented me. He never said something as banal as beautiful.

We went to a small restaurant by the riverside, the service was appalling. I remember being upset with the way they weren't refilling our glasses of water but not having the language to scold them. There was another couple there, about seventy years of age, drinking wine like they had the stomach for it. Their skin was wrinkled like roasted tomatoes. They seemed in love. I told my husband we would be like that someday.

His reaction was odd. He pursed his lips.

'What?' I laughed. 'I'm not calling you old now. Later, someday.'

His eyes watered, but he smiled.

The rest of the meal passed in silence. The food was glorious, so was the wine, but there was a strange tension in the air. It looked like my husband wanted to say something. I pressed him, but he was quiet. After the waitress cleared our cups of tiramisu, he leaned towards me and began.

It took me a long time to understand what my husband was saying. I was unwilling to tune into his words. I had always imagined that I would be the one to let the penny drop, to let slip a secret that might ruin our marriage or change the course of our life together. I could hardly hear anything when he spoke. It was as if someone had put him on mute. I saw his hands move, could tell he had reached over to touch my arm, but I felt numb.

My husband was sick. He had been sick for a long time. He had fallen ill when he was younger, long before he had met me and he had hoped it would never come back again. He had hidden this when he had come home with his uncle and aunty to ask me to get married. He had hidden it even when he had agreed to marry me after my mother's death. He had hidden it when we had Ashu, when we were trying for Mira. When we had Mira.

He thought that if he could ignore it, it wouldn't happen.

'Like when you spot someone you know in a crowd and think that if you can't see them, they can't see you either.' I didn't smile at his attempts at making the situation normal. He continued anyway.

The disease had caught up with him. Over the last year, he had begun to fall sick again. He was weak. He started going to the doctor. He thought it would have gone by now. He tried to tell me many times, but then, look, I was just not myself. I wouldn't get out of bed. I cried at the drop of a hat. I met that guy—what's his name—and my mood went for a toss. I was fighting with everyone. I even began picking fights with the maid! So, how could he tell me? But he should've told me. He knows, he knows, he should have. So, he planned this trip. One last holiday. If we were away from home, the words would come easier to him. He would finally tell me the truth. Because this thing, it had been killing him. Hanging over his head every day, for the past few years, every goddamn fucking day.

He spoke in a fluster and looked like he was going to cry. He tried to touch my hand, but I moved it away.

For a second, I felt an impulse—to tell him the truth about Ashu. To tell him that the son he so loved was never his. This marriage was a lie, a sham. I had never loved him, I could say. I would circle the truth and build lies on top of it, anything to hurt him more than he was hurting me. But before I could, I stopped.

I rose quietly, pushed the chair away from the table and walked out of the restaurant towards the bay. I kept walking, noticing for the first time how dirty Italy was. How unpolished the street lamps, how fat the people. I could feel the crowd overwhelming me in the square and smell the grease floating off stray plates of spaghetti. The smells started to lodge themselves in my throat. I kept walking, when eventually, I heard him again. He was panting. He apologised, tried to take me into his arms.

When he was done crying, I pursed my lips and asked, 'How long?'

He stared at me. He didn't expect me to be so morbid, but I needed to know. I repeated myself. 'How long do you have left?'

'A few months.'

I nodded, feeling a tightness in my chest, red wine and grease trapped within. As I lifted my arms and wrapped them around him tight, I wondered what we looked like to strangers from afar. Both liars, but of a different sort. Both alive, but one soon to be gone.

ASHU

A couple of years ago, Ma had taken Ashu and Mira to a funeral. It was somebody Ma hardly knew, but it was rude to call anyone a stranger when you lived in the same colony, breathed the same air, heard the same sounds of the azaan from the neighbourhood mosque, and come summer, ate the same sickly sweet chikoos. So, Ashu had followed Ma. Everyone was dressed in scratchy white clothes, and the air smelled strong and sweet. Ashu remembered being the only child at the funeral besides Mira. Ma shrugged when someone asked her why she had got the kids with her. Mira spent most of the time there hiding behind Ma's thin georgette dupatta while Ashu chose to focus on a stain on the mattress they were all sitting on cross-legged. He felt out of place there, amidst the adults alternately grieving and chatting, crying and exchanging stories. But then again, Ashu felt like that in most places, shops, school, even home.

After the funeral, Ashu recalled, Mira had become morbidly obsessed with death for a while. Even though she was only six, every second question she asked Ma was related to someone's demise. She wanted to know where people went after they died, and if dying was like taking an afternoon nap, only for a long, long time. She wanted to know if people turned into ghosts immediately after or if there was a waiting period like at the dentist's. She wanted to know if their father had died and if she would too. And when it occurred to her, she wanted to know what another word for death was. 'Moth?' Mira repeated, eyes blinking, when Ma told her.

'Close enough,' Ma said.

Ashu looked on, surprised that Mira had thought of things that he hadn't, even though he was older than her, and he waited for what Ma had to say.

Ma answered some questions, but ignored most, as was her way. She wasn't one to answer a question straight, to tell a truth that wasn't wrapped in a lie.

On the way back from the funeral, too, when Mira and Ashu had gingerly enquired about the way the person they had seen wrapped in white cotton died, Ma said she was old, ate her dinner too fast and choked on her food. Mira, amused, wrapped her grubby fingers around her own neck and made strangulation sounds. Ashu laughed because Ma did, but the image stayed with him for days.

* * *

The day after the kiss, Ashu went to school, desperate to see Rahul. He paced the hallways before the bell rang, hoping to catch him. But Rahul didn't come. Ashu twisted his fingers together all day, feeling a strange vacuum around, because now that he knew what it was like to hold Rahul's hand, his own hands alone felt odd. He could barely focus on what the teacher was saying, he missed his name during attendance. He didn't take down any notes, he forgot to hand in his unfinished holiday homework. How careless it was to give a part of himself to someone else, he thought, even something as small in surface area as the palm of the hand. Not for the first time, all the men Ma had brought home over the years came to his mind. How after each of them eventually left, Ma seemed smaller, frailer, like fragments of herself belonged to someone else now. Is that what it was to fall in love? To lose yourself bit by bit—first your hand, then your heart, then your mind?

'What? Missing your boyfriend?' Ishan joked later in the day. He was sitting on top of Ashu's desk, eating biscuits messily, crumbs falling to the floor. Boys like him would do anything to make themselves appear bigger, Ashu knew. He also knew that the only reason Ishan and the rest of the popular boys tolerated him—or, at least, pretended to be nice to him—was because of Rahul. Whether or not they liked to admit it, they were in awe, maybe even fearful, of him. Perhaps it was Rahul's height, or the fact that Rahul could throw a hefty punch. When he was around, bullies like Ishan kept their tongues neatly rolled up inside their mouths like carpets collecting dust. But they let their words loose when Ashu was alone. It was easier to say a mean word or two, or to leave Ashu behind when they went to play football, and later, smirk and say that they were sorry, man, it was an honest mistake.

Ishan probed him further, but Ashu didn't take the bait. He knew that if he reacted, he would be in as much trouble as if he didn't, so he picked up his lunchbox and sat somewhere else. This was the way it was always going to be, Ashu thought. Others could show off about their girlfriends, kiss them outside school, spill their secrets to the boys around. Ashu, too, could love someone, but he had to be quiet about it. Rahul and he could kiss, or laugh like there was something tickling them in their ears, or even make mistakes like shooting down black birds and leaving them to die—but they had to do it alone, privately, only in the company of a wasp and a whirring fan.

At home, Ashu wolfed down his dal-chawal quickly. He didn't really notice if it was hot or bland or watery or mixed with achaar the way he usually liked it. When he was done, Ma said in a tired voice, 'I said feed yourselves, not absolutely stuff yourselves.' She looked at him as though he weren't just a boy tired after a first day at school, but a hyena in the savannah. Ashu felt prickled by her words, but at least, he thought, she was back to being herself. He waited at the table for Ma and Mira to finish their meals. When they were done, he slid out of his chair, causing an ugly, scraping sound. He ran to his room, grabbing the landline on his way, and closed the door behind him. He felt Mira trying to turn the handle, but he shoved his back against the door. Then he dialled the number he knew best and waited, heart thumping, to ask what had happened and why Rahul wasn't there. He called, then called again. But no one picked up.

When Rahul didn't show at school the following day either, Ashu sat with a heavy feeling in his chest. He struggled to pay attention in class, all the while dreading what could be wrong. That afternoon, he went to Rahul's house after school, climbing the familiar dusty stairs two steps at a time, leaping towards the door. He rang the bell impatiently, and Rahul's mother opened. She liked Ashu. She usually called him in, offered him nimbu pani if it was a hot day. She didn't mind him staying over as long as their house wasn't teeming with relatives. But right now, she stood at the door like a guard. 'Rahul's not well,' she said in a strange, sad voice. Then she shut the door in his face.

On Wednesday, finally, Ashu saw a familiar figure slouch his way through class. He got up quickly, knocking his wooden chair over, and he moved the backpack that he had placed on the seat beside him to the floor. But Rahul walked past him and took a seat in the opposite end of room.

Through English and Maths, Ashu tried to focus on the shapes on the blackboard, but he could only see Rahul from the corner of his eye. He wondered if he could read Rahul's thoughts the way Mira read his. Or if Rahul could read his, could sense how badly

Ashu needed to talk to him, tell him everything he had missed over the past two days—how much he needed to hear that Rahul was okay. He focused on the way Rahul stared out the window, kept his ears to the desk, ruffled his brown hair, buried his head in his hands. But no matter how much Ashu stared, Rahul never once looked back at him.

At the start of lunch, Rahul got up from his seat, walking out of the classroom dully. He even shook his head at Ishan and Manav who had walked up to him with a football.

'Rahul.' Ashu got up from his seat to follow him.

Rahul must not have heard him. Ignoring the crowd that was now gathering in the corridor, Ashu began to walk faster. He called out again, louder, 'Rahul, wait for me.'

Rahul was walking at such a speed now that Ashu had to jog so he didn't lose him. The situation was so ridiculous, Ashu almost wanted to laugh. But he finally caught up with Rahul near the chemistry lab.

There were tears in Rahul's eyes. The bruises on his face had become deeper and looked fresh. His eyes looked saggy. He hadn't been looking good when he had come over the other day but at least he had looked better than this.

'Are you alright?' Ashu said softly.

People were walking past them, looking at them with curiosity. It was as if two boys couldn't speak to each other unless they hit each other and loudly slapped one another's backs.

Ashu reached over to touch him on his shoulders and felt Rahul's back stiffen. He was barely looking at Ashu, and though Ashu couldn't understand why, Rahul almost seemed angry with him.

Not knowing what else to do, Ashu gestured that they keep walking until they were out of the building and had reached a quieter open area of the school. It was the spot where there was a puja every morning to cleanse the school's air of all impurities. Few students came here. There was still smoke, though it had been a couple of hours since the havan had taken place. Ashu's eyes watered, and he squeezed them shut. When he opened his eyes, for a second, he could see tiny invisible worms in the air.

'Rahul.' Ashu walked closer to him, looking around to check no one was listening. 'Please tell me. What happened?'

Rahul didn't respond, only stared into the distance at the large peepal trees.

Ashu swallowed his spit then and asked, 'Is it—your dad?' Ashu's eyes darted towards the bruises on Rahul's face. They seemed to be masked under a layer of makeup and were visible only to him. He moved closer to touch his face. Maybe if he were gentle enough, he could help make it better.

This time, Rahul looked at him, but his eyes seemed cool and hard.

'Forget anything ever happened.'

'Are you talking about—that day?'

Rahul nodded with a jerk.

'You know I won't tell anyone—' Suddenly, Ashu remembered the other evening. The wringing of water. A wasp. A snagged thumb. A kiss. He smiled at Rahul now. 'You know I never would say a word, but can't *we* talk about it?' Rahul was so close to him that again that Ashu felt overwhelmed by the smell of cloves.

'Don't—' Rahul turned away from him, nearly pushing Ashu away.

Ashu stumbled back.

'I mean, you should forget about,' Rahul gestured vaguely at the space between them '—anything. Everything.'

Ashu didn't know what to say.

'Ash,' Rahul said. His voice was kinder now, but it seemed like it belonged to someone else. 'It was a mistake,' Ashu could hear him saying. 'A huge one.'

Ashu once again got the familiar feeling that he was watching his favourite movie but it was being aired in a different language.

'Why are you doing this?' He couldn't help but ask.

Rahul shrugged.

'I thought you liked it—me—the kiss.'

'It was a mistake,' Rahul said again. 'I don't want to do that again. It's not me. I'm not—I'm not the kind of person who does things like that. So, yeah.' He clicked his tongue when Ashu continued to stare at him in disbelief. 'Yeah, I don't want to do this—*that*—again. In fact,' Rahul took a long pause, 'I don't think I want to be friends anymore.'

Ashu could barely believe this was the same Rahul who had held his hand the previous week. The person with the tiger stripes on his back, who buried his head in his hands. Who had reached out for Ashu, who kissed him.

'Please forget about it,' Rahul repeated, and he turned around to go back inside the building as the school bell rang.

Ashu stayed on the grounds long after, thinking about what happened. He was shivering, he realised, but his palms were warm. As he steadied his breath, he spotted a beady-eyed crow staring at him from the tree above. It had large black feathers and seemed to be mocking him, its caws growing in intensity. At first, he tried to ignore it, but as the sound got louder, Ashu looked around. No one was watching. He found a large rock on the ground and aimed it straight at the bird.

CHOKE

MIRA

This is how Ma wears a sari—she takes a cloth and twists around it tight like she's a hurricane. Then she folds it up like a harmonium that goes in-out-in-out. She presses her tummy like it's aching and does a long sigh in the mirror. When she sees that Ashu or I are around her, she flips around and asks, 'How am I looking?' Then even if we go through the good list of compliments that Ma likes to hear and say that she's looking lovely or exquisite or even hot, like I once heard her say to herself, she changes out of the sari and tries another one, doing the whole thing all over again.

Usually Ma is not the type of person to wear a sari at all. She likes clothes that Ashu and I do—trousers and shorts and dresses that go way beyond the knees and scrub the floor. But these days is not Usually, it's, as Ma says, Wedding Season. Which I have to say doesn't sound like a real season like summer or monsoon at all, but instead like a time when Ma leaves the house for long hours and comes back looking unhappy. Ma said that when you add the word 'un' to some words it becomes the opposite. So, when Ashu says that I eat more sweets than him, it's untrue. And when Ma has a fight with someone on the road, she mutters, 'Unbelievable!' And when on her birthday we go and make a mountain hug on top of her as she's sleeping and give her a cake made with Mrs Shome's help, she says, 'Unnecessary!' But I can see she's smiling really.

When Ma goes out, she doesn't look so much like Ma with a mole on her chin but like a movie actress with her hair all big and fluffy and long red nails. She tips and toes to the cupboard and takes out a necklace that makes her neck sparkle. And before she leaves, she does acting with Ashu and me.

Ma: Oh, hello, Mrs Chandra!

Us: Hello, Ma! How are you? (And Ma corrects us and makes us call her by her real name.)

Ma: I'm well, thanks. Work's fab and, um, everything else too.

Us: Might we add—you look gorgeous today!

Ma (throws her head back and laughs): Haha.

Us: What about your husband? Any man in the picture yet?

Ma (straightening her head): Not everyone needs a husband, Mrs Chandra. Now I'd best be going and getting a drink, don't you think?

Then she waves and waves at us, like she's going out of the room and she isn't coming back ever.

ASHU

'Ma, please. No.'

Ma raised her eyebrows high. It wasn't often that Ashu said that word to her, and he could tell that he had enraged her. He tried to return her stare defiantly, but Ma no longer seemed to be focusing on Ashu. Instead, she appeared disoriented and wouldn't meet his gaze. His eyes darted around the room, and he noticed a round glass bottle with a black sticker and a fat base under Ma's bed. The glass of the bottle looked dark and dirty, with no light passing through it. He took a step closer to Ma. She smelt like rum and flowers.

'Why don't you go with Coach instead?' he tried again.

Ma's voice slurred slightly and her gait staggered. '*Why don't you go with Coach instead?*' She mimicked Ashu, then said in her own voice, 'If I knew where Coach was, I would've gone with him. I don't *like* to take kids to weddings. I'm not an idiot.'

Mira, who had just entered the room, was dressed in an orange lehenga, her short black hair brushed at odd angles. Was that lipstick? Ashu wondered as she came towards him and held his hand. Ashu wrinkled his brows. Her palms were clammy. And there was definitely something jam-like on her mouth. She appeared to have borrowed some of Ma's makeup. Ma didn't notice. She clearly wasn't in a state to.

Looking between Ma and Mira, he felt torn between resentment and responsibility. Although it wasn't her fault, Ashu sometimes felt that Mira had no idea how easy she had it with Ma. Something about them just clicked. When he saw Ma and Mira together, he thought, that's right. That's an image that fits. It was a feeling he himself had never had. There was always an unease between him and Ma, an unsung truth hanging from a low branch of a tree, almost touching the palm of his hand but always just slightly out of reach.

When he was little, he used to put all his energy into trying to figure out what would make Ma happy. He shape-shifted his personality every other week. Tried to mould himself to a version that Ma would like. He eventually picked this one. He turned from loud to quiet, from active to passive, from present to barely there, and though he realised that Ma didn't love this version of him either, it seemed acceptable to her. Mira had never felt like that, he was sure. She'd never have to.

Still, looking at Ma first, and then down at Mira's hand, her fingers painted untidily in pink with Ma's nail polish, he felt a tenderness tug at him. This person holding his hand was an extension of him. He didn't have a choice.

'Fine,' he said, sighing, and he went to his cupboard to pull an old kurta over his head; it had a small tear around its armhole that Ma had said she would fix but hadn't. 'Fine,' he said again. 'Let's go.'

In the car, when Mira asked if she could sit in front, Ashu didn't put up a fight. His thoughts had moved far beyond the scope of family matters. It had been almost a week since Rahul had stopped talking to him. A week since they had kissed. If Ashu had known that doing that would alter the course of their friendship forever, he wouldn't have done it. Wouldn't have asked to kiss him, wouldn't have leaned in further, wouldn't have held his hand. But it wasn't Ashu who had asked first, was it? It was Rahul.

The more Ashu tried to remember the sequence of events that led to the kiss, the more jumbled up they seemed to get, and the only thing he was left with was a small ache in the middle of his chest. If it were up to him right now, he'd be sitting by the phone in case Rahul tried to reach him. But Ma had other plans.

'Who is getting wedded?' Ashu heard Mira ask Ma from the front seat.

Ma let out a howl. 'Wedded! You really crack me up, Mira.' Then she gathered herself and said, 'Some people I work with.' She must have seen Mira open her mouth because she said, 'No more questions, Mira. Come, let's practise.'

Ashu groaned inwardly as his sister and Ma began: 'Oh, hello, Mrs—'

Ashu wasn't in the mood to participate today. He mouthed his part half-heartedly from the back of the car until they reached the destination, wondering if all families in the world were as mad as his.

* * *

Ashu had never been to anything like this before. Everyone seemed to be wearing shiny clothes. There were so many people—and all of them looked beautiful, like they were movie actresses, maybe even more beautiful than Ma.

Much like Ashu, Ma and Mira looked stumped as they entered, though Ma quickly rearranged her face and walked through the wedding grounds like it had been hers all along. At one end, there was a stage decked with flowers where the bride and groom were sitting. Mira pointed to the ornamental lights hanging from the tree branches to Ashu, but he was looking above them. There were bats flying over the trees. He was sure no one else could see them, but to Ashu, they were there, clear as day, circling high over the trays of appetisers.

'Ma,' Ashu clutched his chest. 'I feel—'

He felt uneasy and he didn't know why.

But Ma had already walked on ahead like she had forgotten that she had, just an hour ago, arm-twisted him into coming along to this event. Even Mira was not able to catch up with her and she kept stumbling on the grass in her shoes.

Ashu whispered to ask if Mira wanted to eat something. One good thing about this place was that it was overflowing with food and drinks. Plates of cocktail samosas, fish fry and seekh kebabs were floating by, all marked with little green and red circles to indicate if they contained meat. Ashu stopped the servers passing by to scoop up handfuls of the appetisers into tissues using toothpicks, along with the accompanying green chutney. When the food was consumed and the chutney seeped into the tissues, he curled the papers into a ball and threw it away.

In the meantime, Ma had finally stopped storming ahead. From the corner of his eye, Ashu could see that she had caught up with some aunties. Maybe they were her colleagues. They all looked much older than Ma, and they all had men—presumably their husbands—standing beside them. Ashu walked closer.

One woman, who was wearing bright red lipstick, looked over Ma's shoulder and enquired, 'Has your instructor not come?'

Another woman wearing a lot of gold jewellery laughed.

Ashu felt Ma visibly tighten her shoulder. She slurred, 'Coach.'

The red-lipped woman by this time had turned to her husband and was asking him something privately. But Ma continued talking, wagging her finger at the whole group. 'And he's better than any of these fat pouches you all call husbands.'

Ashu darted Mira a look. The women laughed feebly like they didn't know what to do. They quickly moved away, the group scattering, becoming small fragments. It wasn't just him, Ashu realised for the first time. No one wanted to be around Ma when she got mean.

The three of them now walked towards the buffet area, which was a procession of stainless-steel chafing dishes. Ma was ravenous and filled her plate up to a heap before carrying it to a round table nearby. It took everything in Ashu's willpower not to mock her or tell her that it was she who was the monster this time. But at least with each thing Ma ate, she seemed to return closer to her sober self. Ashu was grateful for that.

When she was done, she held her plate up towards Ashu.

Mira got up to help, but Ma held her down. '*No*, I asked *him*.'

Ashu went to put Ma's empty plate away, but as he walked back, he saw that she wasn't alone. Someone else had joined their table.

Although Ashu couldn't see the man's face, he could tell that he was someone who thought a lot of himself. His back was too straight, and he was standing with his arms crossed, looking at the table and at Ma and Mira. All of them seemed to be engaged in serious conversation.

It was when Ashu actually reached the table that he realised that Ma was quiet, and it was only the man who was speaking.

'—lad I'm not puking at your doorstep this time, eh? And is that your daughter?' he was saying.

It was an innocent statement, but Ma seemed to shrivel up. Then she saw Ashu, and her face fell.

The man must have seen that because he turned sideways to Ashu to include him in the conversation. Putting his arm around him, the stranger said, 'You must be Ashish.'

'Ashu,' he replied in a clipped voice. Ashu wasn't sure who this man was and why he was being this familiar with him. He tried to remove the weight of this stranger's arm, free himself of it, but the man wouldn't budge.

'Heard so much about Leela's kids. And you're a particularly handsome boy. Has anyone told you that?'

Ashu's head was hurting, and it didn't help that this person wouldn't stop talking. He shook his head.

The man now swivelled Ashu towards him so they were standing face to face. Ashu looked up at him. He had his deep brown eyes and Ashu felt like he was looking at something he'd seen once—maybe in an old movie, maybe in a dream—but he couldn't place a finger on it.

'People will realise it when you're older. Believe me. Used to be friends with your mother. She was a star.'

From the corner of his eye, Ashu saw Ma place a finger on her head like she was having a splitting headache. 'Please,' she said, but it didn't seem like a request. Ma sounded like she was physically writhing in pain. 'Please don't,' she said softly.

The noises around them were rising. Ashu felt like he was in the ocean and waves were crashing all over him. Everything got heightened at once—the low, lyrical music, the twinkling lights, the increasingly cool air. Ashu noticed that his younger sister too had gotten up and sidled closer to Ma. She was suspicious of any man who spoke to Ma longer than was necessary.

Ma coughed. She seemed to want to end the conversation. Ashu did too. He couldn't pinpoint what it was, but the man seemed to smile from the corner of his mouth, the way people do when they don't mean what they are saying. Who was he again? Ashu wondered idly, but Ma got up from her chair.

'Let's go,' she muttered to Ashu and Mira in a voice so low that if Ashu hadn't recognised it as the same voice that Ma used from underneath her blanket on cloudless days, he might not have heard it at all. She grabbed their hands aggressively and began walking, almost marching, towards the exit.

The people around them were multiplying by hundreds, thousands. Were there that many of them when they first arrived? A deep, sweet sound of a conch being blown sounded far off at a distance, signifying that the wedding rituals were beginning. It continued ringing in Ashu's ears minutes after it ended. He tried to slow down to catch his breath. But Ma had a tight grip on him. This must be what a snakebite feels like, he thought.

As they merged with the crowds, Ashu felt it again. A tightening of the chest, a sudden hit of breathlessness. Trees, that were not there a second earlier, began racing towards him, whooshing fast over his head to form a canopy, thick and green. He tried to reach out, extend his arm to grab the branches and steady himself, but he couldn't. It was the last thing he remembered before his knees buckled onto the grass, and the world slowly faded in front of him.

It was a while before Ma and Mira realised that Ashu wasn't with them; a while before people finally looked down to the ground and saw him lying there, eyes shut and face smudged with dirt. For a moment, they all believed that the boy was dead.

Death was an inconvenience I wasn't interested in. I had seen it happen before, I didn't care for it at all. I spurred myself into action after Italy. Replaced my feelings with footsteps, put a stopper on emotion with movement. I kept my husband in bed for the most part. At all other times, we made the rounds of hospitals. We moved so fast, from one corridor to the other, that everything became a blur of chemists, medicines, doctors. I hated going to the hospital, with the bright white lights that lent unpleasantness to an already grim situation. I would grasp my husband's hand tightly throughout the visits, seemingly to give him support, but in reality, it was I who was shaking. I even considered praying for his health, but I knew from past experience that this would be useless. It hadn't helped my mother. It wouldn't help me.

Now that things in life finally felt stable, I wanted to protect them. We had proved to the world that we could be happy. Now it was time to keep it that way. At the first sign of an earthquake, I wanted to shelter my family from the aftershocks. Maybe if the four of us stayed under a common roof, crouched beneath a desk, we could survive this. Ashu could try to run away or Mira could cry or my husband could wobble from weakness, but as long as I gathered us all together—as long as I extended my arm and pulled everyone back under the desk—we would be okay.

I didn't want to, but I called my sister a couple of times. She was overenthusiastic in her desire to help; she kept calling Ashu a handsome boy. I pushed Mira before her when she visited. Look, this is my child, I wanted to say. I hoped she would be able to see the truth. But she understood nothing.

Since I needed help with the children, I left them with her and her kid sometimes. She asked questions, but I gave clipped responses. I didn't want to let her in entirely.

The doctors were arrogant, convinced that they knew everything. No matter where we went, they looked at us with sympathetic eyes, tried to hide their verdicts by dropping heavy euphemisms. They used medical words that went over both our heads. Even though I asked questions to untangle the complicated phrases they used, I found all their responses puzzling.

It wasn't the first time that I had regretted not finishing college. Or studying something as impractical as literature for the little while that I did. What good were books when your loved one was dying? What good were they when your bills were sky-rocketing and the money was drying up?

There were days when I had to wait at home for the doctor's secretary to call up with test results. The children would be asleep, and I would sit by the phone for hours and read. I'd go through the books I had accumulated over time. Some of them were stacked inside my bedside drawer. Some were laid flat underneath the mattress. Sometimes, I'd get annoyed with the writing. If there were too many adjectives or lengthy paragraphs describing trees, I'd throw the book away in frustration. But occasionally, a book would grab my attention. I wouldn't realise it—when I'd grow invested in the story, when the words would translate into images, when the hours would pass and the light outside would shift. For that time, I wouldn't think about anything: not him, not me, not the past or the future. Maybe this is all literature can do. Maybe this is enough.

As the weeks passed, my husband started taking up less space in the bed. I sometimes got the irrational thought that he would sprint out the door and just leave us forever. It didn't make sense. My husband could hardly walk, let alone run. Still, rationality was an alien concept to me at that point. I began staying awake to keep an eye on him, to make sure he wouldn't go. I bought a small bedside lamp and sat upright most nights, so I wouldn't get tempted to sleep. One night, however, I accidentally fell into a deep slumber and woke up at two, maybe three in the morning with a start. I spread my fingers lightly on the silk bedcover we had been gifted for our wedding and felt a blank space next to me. I couldn't believe it, he wasn't there.

I got up immediately, switched on all the lights and started searching the flat. I still remember a sense of calm in my mind even though my actions were chaotic. I threw open cupboards as though he would be hiding there, shouted his name while I walked around with heavy footsteps. When I remembered the sleeping children, I dropped my voice to a low but frantic whisper. Eventually, I found him in the kitchen, next to the refrigerator. He was lying near the cold, open door, his arms sprawled above his head. He told me later that he must have fainted after getting up for a glass of cold water. His face was white. To me, he looked feeble. He said my name, but it was barely a murmur. He wasn't dead, but he was already a ghost.

* * *

It was a warm Sunday. Sunlight was streaming in through the window in soft, gentle waves and my husband was happy. We had had so many sleepless nights in a row that I was too exhausted to question why. 'Come back,' he groaned when I leapt out of bed to get him his medicines. I obliged, confused by this abrupt surge in energy. We spent the day in bed, lightly wrapping ourselves around each other. I rested my head on his, and he laced his fingers in mine. I had learned to be so careful around him over the past two weeks that even now I held my weight in my stomach as I leaned on him. He could feel it, and he pulled me closer. 'You've been carrying too much,' he said, and I let go.

We spent the rest of the day like that. We even let Mira and Ashu into our bed. Ashu kept giggling. He had imagined up a person he called Gigi, and he kept referring to her as his friend. What a silly name, I thought. Throughout the day, he kept shoving her off, telling her that he had to be with his family now. He seemed utterly convinced that this other little person existed; he was talking to her even when we were huddled up together. I found his behaviour concerning and thought Mira would learn odd things from her brother. I made a mental note to talk to my husband about it later but tucked the thought away.

That night, after I put the kids to bed, my husband and I slid under the quilt. We began to kiss. It had been several weeks since we had touched each other. He insisted that he was feeling up to it and shoved away my concerns. He unbuttoned my shirt and began to kiss my neck like he used to when we first got married. I went with it. How could I tell him that I was tired when he was the one who was sick? When it came to it, though, he couldn't actually do it. 'It must be the medicines,' he said in a low, disappointed voice. I kissed him on his cheek.

'Tomorrow,' I winked at him. 'You'll make it up to me tomorrow.'

When my husband went to sleep, I turned on the bedside lamp, cracked open a book and prepared myself to stay on guard for the night. I barely knew when I drifted off, too.

My dreams felt like quicksand. I kept falling deeper, more uncontrollably into them. One moment, I was on the bed; the next, I was at my parents' home with my mother, the air full of a strange, strong burning smell. I wanted to spend time with my mother. I saw her in the puja room ringing the ghanti, her sari wrapped tightly around her, but just as I decided to open my mouth to say something, I found myself gone. This time, I was with Ashu. We were laughing, and I seemed to be strangely, deliriously happy. I was holding Ashu and walking on the beach. We were collecting shells, thousands of them, tiny, gorgeous shells in our palms. Where's Mira, I sometimes wondered. She might enjoy this. But the air was so cool that I kept forgetting about her. Her name kept escaping me. I held Ashu's tiny, rough hand, and we ran towards the shore. He was trying to tickle me, and I was laughing. It was only when a cloud burst that I opened my eyes to see a window had thrown itself open. I got out of bed quickly to shut it. This made a loud sound, and I looked over to check that my husband hadn't woken up. He was still sleeping peacefully.

'You won't believe it,' I said, slipping back into bed, turning off the lamp and tugging at the blanket to cover my feet. 'The neighbour—' But I felt strange. I patted the mattress around me and realised the bed was wet. I turned the lamp back on again to see how the rain had made its way in. But it wasn't the rain. It was him.

People make dying in your sleep sound peaceful, luxurious. They make you want to hope for it, even wish for it. They don't talk about how the dying slowly lose their sense of self as they sleep. They don't talk about the loss of control over bowel movements, the weak stream of yellow urine that soaks the mattress.

I could have helped him. I could have taken him to the doctor, given him some medicines, injections—anything to help. Or if it were time for him to go, I could at least have been awake, to notice him flinching, twitching in his sleep. To see to him, kiss him, hold him, say goodbye.

Had he tried to call out to me? I hadn't heard him.

Ashu had dragged me in my dreams, and now, I had lost my husband. Not for the first time, Ashu had ruined my life.

ASHU

When Ashu finally opened his eyes, he felt startlingly calm, like he had just dipped his head underwater for a moment. He had been having dreams, but they were no stranger than usual. Two mynahs were swooping down to the ground and flying back to the sky, but one of them kept flying faster and faster till the other gave up.

Ashu tried to turn on his side but a sharp twinge in his arm stopped him. He blinked open his eyes and saw that he was no longer lying on grass, nor was he in the middle of a dream. He was in Ma's room. He knew by the patch on the wall that was damp.

People were trying to whisper around him. That was Ma's voice. The other one was familiar too. Soft, reassuring, husky. Mrs Shome.

'He seemed to be gone,' said Ma.

'What do you mean *gone*?'

'It was like—he wasn't there anymore. We tried waking him up, but he just wouldn't respond. I thought he wasn't breathing. Thank god you came.'

Ashu realised that the voices were coming from behind him.

'Why were you alone?' Ashu heard Mrs Shome say after a pause. 'Weren't you going to the wedding with him?'

Ma mumbled something.

'What?' Mrs Shome said sharply.

'I don't know. I haven't seen him.' Ma sounded tired now. 'For a while.'

'Hmm.'

Ashu wanted to open his mouth to tell Ma about seeing Coach at the club. But then he would have to talk about being there. And then he would have to talk about Rahul. A new kind of pain unrelated to his fall rose in Ashu's chest. He jammed his mouth shut.

'Maybe I can't—' Ma's voice broke. Then she steadied herself. 'Maybe I need a break,' she said more clearly.

'What do you mean, Leela?' Mrs Shome's voice was softer now, like she was scolding Ashu or Mira.

'Can I leave the kids with you for a while? Just until I figure some stuff out.'

'Leela—'

Ma's voice stiffened. 'It's fine.'

'You know I'm here to help you, but I can't take on the responsibility. I just got done with raising my own children after—after thirty years. And all *this*—' Then realizing that Ashu was in the room, even if seemingly unconscious, she lowered her voice. 'This needs attention, your attention, Leela. *You* have to take care of it.'

Ma said, 'Of course. Right. Don't worry about it. Forget I said anything.' The weight on the bed shifted as she got up. 'I think we should all get some rest, Anita.' Her voice sounded like a blast from the air conditioner.

There was silence, then Mrs Shome must have got up and walked out the room because the next thing Ashu heard was the front door shutting. Ma entered the room again. Ashu shut his eyes even tighter so Ma wouldn't be able to tell that he was awake, that he had been listening. His heart was beating so loud that it was in his ear. He was surprised Ma couldn't hear it too. He heard Ma lie down next to him, sigh and switch off the light.

* * *

The reasons for not going to school were genuine at first. Ashu had landed straight on to his elbow when he fell. The doctor announced that Ashu seemed to have got a fracture in the arm. He said it as though he were announcing the weekly weather ('a dip in temperature') or that the Boeing to Kolkata would take off an hour late ('a delay in the flight'). Ashu, when he heard the doctor, felt like the fracture didn't belong to him but to a stray arm in a white cast, floating away in space towards the unknown.

After a scan, it turned out it was just a bad sprain. The painkillers the doctor prescribed were surprisingly helpful. They had a side effect that wasn't mentioned on the silver foil print. They gave Ashu a dreamless sleep. There were no strange people hijacking Ashu's dreams now, no faceless women, no bees, no wasps, no kisses with boys. If Ma left the medicine by his bed by mistake, Ashu would take a pill quickly even if he had just had his dose and put the strip back before she returned.

In the days that followed, Mrs Shome came home often to visit him. She brought adventure books that Ashu would never read and an assortment of Indian sweets and pastries that he had to share with Mira. Mrs Shome and Ma continued to talk coldly to each other. The last time she was over, they barely said a word to one another, but at least, Ashu thought with relief, that didn't make Mrs Shome stop loving them.

A few days later, there was a visitor. Ashu had been lying down, throwing a ball at the wall with the arm that didn't ache, when the doorbell rang and Ma called out his name. He had been waiting for this moment for days, and now that it had arrived, he threw the covers off himself and got up, brushing his hair back with his fingers as quickly as he could. He felt his knees shake, and he took a breath in. Cool and composed. That's what he would be.

When he looked up at who it was, he sat back down with a jerk. It was Ishan.

Ishan, too, looked like he was surprised to be there, as though he had made the decision on the spur of the moment, and now that he was here at Ashu's place, he didn't know what to do with himself. He had come straight from school. His striped blue-and-white shirt was crinkled like abandoned computer paper, and his black shoes were muddied from football, no doubt. He stood at the door of Ashu and Mira's room, clutching on to the straps of his schoolbag.

'Hi,' Ashu said, awkwardly. 'Thanks for, er, coming.'

Ishan nodded. It was a small jerk of a movement, and it was difficult to gauge what it meant. He entered the room.

'Here.' Ma came in and handed a glass of water to Ishan. She looked down at his feet. 'You really should take your shoes off before entering someone's home.' Ashu turned red. Was Ma scolding Ishan right now? Did she know she was talking to the most popular boy in ninth grade? She left and closed the door behind them with a click.

Ishan took a seat at the edge of Ashu's bed and set the glass down.

Ashu had never been alone with Ishan. They had only ever spent time in the company of others. They had smoked together, been around each other in the classroom with horizontal rows of desks separating them. But seeing him now in the same place where Ashu sat, ate and slept was odd. He looked distorted outside the confines of school. Smaller, shorter somehow. Ashu suddenly wanted to laugh, although nothing was funny. Nothing had been funny for a while.

'Heard you got a cast,' said Ishan finally. 'Can I see it?'

Ashu displayed his cast-less arm.

Ishan scratched his face. 'People thought you died or something.'

'Sorry to disappoint.'

Ishan laughed, pleasantly to Ashu's surprise, then stopped.

They sat for some time without talking, and Ashu wondered why he was here. Seeing Ishan up close out of school had already stopped feeling strange to him. Now Ashu just felt sad. Unable to take the silence, he asked, 'How was school?'

'Good. Good, yeah. Some of the guys missed you.'

'Did they?' Ashu leaned forward with interest.

'Yeah.' Ishan looked away, like he was not supposed to say anything but couldn't help himself. 'Yeah, they really wanted you to know—uh—that they want you to get better soon.'

'Oh,' said Ashu, not knowing what to think. 'Okay. Thanks for letting me know.'

When Ishan responded with a shrug, Ashu spoke once again. 'So—are they okay, then? The class?'

He nodded, not quite looking Ashu in the eye. 'Yup. As okay as can be.' Ishan began to get up to leave.

Ashu felt confused at the roundaboutness of this conversation, and his arm ached. He looked away, then spotted at the back of his chair a sweatshirt he had once borrowed. He felt irritated, but he didn't want Ishan to go away just yet.

'Why—' he said. 'Why are you here anyway?'

Ishan looked at him blankly and stood awkwardly by the door.

'The two of you are the most unlikely friends ever.' Ashu gave a bitter laugh. 'You're always hurting people. You're such a coward. I still don't understand why Rahul hangs out with you.'

'Coward?' Ishan said, eyes narrowing. 'Is that what you think of me?'

'That's what everybody thinks of you.'

For a moment, Ashu imagined that Ishan would slam the door and leave. Perhaps, he'd even throw a punch at Ashu, now that nobody was there to stop him. Instead, Ishan took a deep breath in and walked back into the room.

'Why are you so angry?' he asked.

Ashu was stunned. He blurted out, 'People like you—you act so above it all. You bully people into being friends with you, you take advantage of them, get them into trouble and don't care what happens to—'

'Ashu.'

Ashu was startled when he heard his name. He realised with shame that until that point Ishan had only ever addressed him with profanities.

Ishan, who didn't seem to notice the shift in Ashu's expression, continued. 'Do you actually think I have to bully people for company? Has Rahul ever told you how we became friends?'

'Well—I,' Ashu scratched his head. 'Didn't you—there was something about being on the same bus or—no,' he said finally. 'He didn't.'

Ishan sat back down on Ashu's bed. It was so surreal to have him there, to hear him tell stories which were probably untrue, that Ashu suddenly thought that if *this* could happen, anything could—summer could overnight turn into winter, he could rank first in class, Ma could start loving him over Mira, his voice could finally break.

Ishan began. 'Remember Maan?'

'No.'

'Well, a few years ago, Maan and his brother from the senior batch were a bit, let's say, unfriendly.'

Ashu raised his eyebrows.

'Okay, fine, they were goons. There wasn't a person they didn't have beef with. You didn't want to mess with them. They were also extremely controlling. Used to consider themselves the unassigned monitors of the school. I was cool with them, of course. I knew them from before—from our neighbourhood. We used to hang out.

'They were messing around looking for people who were—' Ishan looked uncomfortable again, '—different, I guess. One day, they called me to help bully this person. When I got there, it was Rahul.'

Ashu continued to listen, his mouth agape.

'I recognised Rahul from class obviously. Some of the seniors from school had heard rumours about him. Maan and his brother were calling Rahul names, threatening to beat him up. They were almost about to punch Rahul's face, but I stepped in—stopped a big brawl from breaking out. The seniors were passing out of school that year, so the matter folded pretty quickly. Since then Rahul and I have been cool, I guess.'

Ashu stared at him. This was not the version of the story he knew. 'What rumours?' he asked, in spite of himself and in spite of the fact that there was a good chance that Ishan was lying through his teeth. 'And why would Rahul need *your* help? He's stronger and braver than you,' Ashu spat the words out bitterly.

'I'm not too surprised Rahul didn't tell you anything of this.' Ishan clicked his tongue.

Ashu felt that Ishan was restraining himself from saying something, but he wasn't sure what.

'Maybe you aren't the first person Rahul's been close to,' Ishan said finally, giving him a strange smile. 'Maybe Rahul's not as brave as you think.'

Ishan suddenly got up. It was as though he had reached the end of his script and didn't know what else to say. He plunged his hand into his schoolbag and tossed Ashu a book. 'This is for you. You should take a look. So you don't stop being a nerd.'

Ashu took a quick glance at it. It was their maths homework. 'Thanks,' he said, keeping it aside.

Ishan finally left.

Ashu was left feeling drained from the interaction. He sank back into the bed, closing his eyes. Briefly, he felt something on his bed. It was the notebook. Algebra. He tossed it aside, the medicine taking control of him, and fell asleep.

When he woke up a few hours later, the house was fully dark. Where was everyone? The windows weren't shut, and dust motes were swirling in the air. Ma must have forgotten to turn on the lights like she usually did in the evenings. He could hear a few people murmuring from the street below, the evening call from the mosque, a guard cycling slowly on his way back from work, stopping to call out to a friend he met on the way.

Ashu's arm ached, and his mouth felt dry. He pulled himself out of bed and had a few sloppy sips of water. Walking around the house now, he called out for Mira, then Ma, then Mira again. They must have gone to the market. Or maybe Ma had stopped by Coach's. Ashu turned on the lights, made himself a snack and ate it. He added some of Ma's ground coffee to a cup of boiling water. Holding the cup, he sat down on the floor and started thinking about that afternoon with Ishan. How strange it was to see him here at home. It was like seeing a teacher in the mall, or like watching the news—a report flashing that there was a leopard on the highway.

Ashu left the kitchen and started going through the homework with his free hand. There would be a lot of catching up to do when he went back to class, Ashu thought dully. He turned a few pages and browsed through the notes. Ishan had *terrible* handwriting. Despite his sullen mood, Ashu felt compelled to laugh. Seriously, it looked like ants had died and had had a funeral on the page.

He looked through some more of the homework, not because he had developed a sudden love of algebra but because it was fascinating to hold something that belonged to one of the most popular boys at school. Ashu could tell that Ishan really needed some after-school tuitions. As he was thumbing the stained pages, Ashu came across a note neatly tucked into the notebook's spine. He did a double take. He wasn't sure if he was meant to open it, but his curiosity got the better of him. He set his cup of coffee down on the floor and unfolded the square of paper.

Ashu, please meet me at school at seven today

The handwriting here was different, and Ashu recognised it well as Rahul's. He got up quickly, knocking the cup over. The coffee was still hot and scalded his knee, but he didn't register it. He glanced quickly at the clock. It was twenty minutes past seven, but maybe he could still make it.

As Ashu ran down the stairs, his heart thumped wildly. It didn't matter that it was raining and slippery. Or that Ma would get home and walk around with that disappointed, low seething rage of hers and wonder why he hadn't put the milk left on the counter by Ma back in the fridge or why he had left the lights on in his room.

Ashu had never made enemies with the rain. Even though it tended to slip in through their windows in the middle of the night, he liked it, found its hammering, consistent sound comforting. He had stared at it, loved the smell of it, took walks in it when he found the house claustrophobic. It was beautiful to him.

But right then, it was a goddamn pain in the ass.

He was ignored and rejected by a few autos even though it was just a light drizzle. No one wanted to travel towards the school. He looked for a bus, an auto, a taxi, anything with wheels. He finally found a hapless driver who probably took pity on him but charged extra for the trip anyway.

When Ashu finally got to the school, it was pitch dark. There was exactly one security guard in uniform who walked lazily past the gate, thumping his fake—Ashu hoped—gun on the ground.

Ashu hung back and waited as inconspicuously as he could. The guard eventually wandered off for his dinner break, and Ashu made a dash for it.

It was strange and dangerous and exciting to rush through the dark school corridors at night. The same place, which was usually a hunting ground for teachers to prey on boys and girls, was now his jungle alone. Ashu felt his heart thud in anticipation as he leapt, his sprint giant and long, stretched out like a leopard's. He rushed to the classroom he usually sat in. He felt tall and invincible. He felt brave.

When he suddenly halted, his bravery shifted shape and settled down, like people in an auditorium after the curtain lifts. He was here. He had finally reached. He walked to his usual seat by the window and suddenly wasn't sure what to expect. Why had Rahul asked him to come and meet him in the school of all places? The place where they hid who they were during the day—could that be the place that allowed them to be themselves at night?

He was still dazed by Ishan's unexpected visit earlier. What had he meant when he had said that Ashu wasn't the first person Rahul had been close to? He had to have been making things up. But his eyes looked so clear.

Maybe he wasn't lying.

Ashu didn't dare to turn on the lights or switch on the fan. He sat, surrounded by thick, unmoving air.

Not for the first time that summer, he waited for Rahul. He traced patterns on the edge of the desk. He drummed against the splintering wood. He tried not to think.

An hour passed and no one came. At some point, Ashu thought he heard footsteps and sat up straight in excitement. It was the guard with a flashlight, casting long shadows on the walls. Ashu ducked until he disappeared and eventually decided to leave. Maybe he had read the note too late and missed Rahul. Maybe he had misunderstood it. Maybe, Ashu realised with a sinking feeling, Rahul had never come at all.

It occurred to Ashu that soon enough, he would have to return to this room in daylight. His arm would heal and Ma would eventually see through his farce and run out of sympathy for him. And then he'd have to see Rahul, in this very classroom, and it would do nothing short of break his heart.

When Ashu stepped outside, he saw that it had started raining more heavily. If it had been hard to find a rickshaw earlier, it would be impossible now. The rain was coming down in sheets. He could feel the weight of the water on his back, could sense the dullness in his arm. Trying to remember the last time he had been warm, with a full stomach, Ashu began to walk home. He shook his head. He had been a fool to come.

Now that he was at his door again, Ashu could hear the TV. Ma and Mira would be laughing, happy, cosy. They would probably be cuddled up together and they—

The door opened.

'Who is skulking outside?' Ma took one look at Ashu and said, 'You. Where were *you*? And *why* are you dripping wet?'

Mira, who was sitting at one end of the sofa, looked at him and widened her eyes. She was trying to give him some sort of a signal, but Ashu was too hungry to care. He walked past Ma and went straight into his room without answering her questions, slamming the door shut. He didn't even remove his muddy shoes. Whatever taunts Ma wanted to throw at him could wait. Right now, he was wet and miserable and wanted to change out of his soaked clothes. He saw, on the floor, the notebook he had been browsing through earlier and kicked it under the bed.

When he went back to the living room, he heated some aloo paranthas and nudged Mira to move over on the sofa. He ate one bite, then another, and slowly felt warmth return to his stomach, to the tips of his fingers. Realizing how late it actually was, he turned to Mira and whispered, 'Why are you still up, silly?' It was past her usual bedtime.

She shrugged.

Ma must not have noticed the time.

'Did you have your medicine?' Ma asked Ashu and sighed. She didn't wait for his response. She seemed restless. Like she didn't know whether to be concerned or annoyed, upset or sad. Ashu changed the TV channel.

That's when the telephone rang.

Ashu and Mira swapped glances. Ma usually told people off if they called past a certain time. But right now, Ma yanked the phone from the receiver and spoke into the mouthpiece. Balancing the phone between her shoulder and her ear, she snatched the television remote from Ashu's hand and began racing through the different channels so quickly that Ashu wondered if she could really even see anything. To him, it was just a blur of colours.

Ma finally paused when she recognised something and increased the volume. Her face, Ashu noticed, had turned white.

Wondering what Ma was watching, he peered at the screen. It was a news channel. There was a debate on TV between two politicians. Ashu couldn't recognise the one who was bald, but the other was a man whose posters Ashu had seen taped to walls all over the city. 'Chauvinist,' Ma usually muttered when he saw his face. But right now, instead of switching off the TV, Ma increased the volume and sat up straight. She gripped the TV remote tightly, turning pale like a ghost. Then she let out a wail as though in pain.

Ashu got to his feet. 'What happened, Ma? Are you okay?' he asked. But Ma just pointed at the TV wordlessly.

'The debate?' Ashu looked at her in surprise.

'Below that,' she said. She sounded sick.

Ashu looked carefully at the screen. Nearly three-fourths of it was taken up by ads, and right at the bottom there was a thin yellow strip with words flashing on it. It said '—mming coach arrested for allegedly molesting 14-year-old, having child porn. Local swimming coach arrested for allegedly—'

'It was a mother from the club—on the phone.' Ma was speaking to no one in particular. 'She thinks—' Her voice broke. 'She thinks it's Coach.'

'What does that mean?' he asked Ma.

He tried to focus on the words floating past him, but even as he read them out in his head, he could tell it was something terrible. Coach. He had never seen anyone from real life on TV before, but this wasn't how he had imagined his first brush with celebrity. Not sure how to respond, Ashu lowered the volume of the TV.

For a few seconds, the only sounds were of the cars passing on the road outside and a low mumbling sound from the television set. Ashu turned it off.

'Oh my god,' Ma finally said, slinking down to the floor. 'What have I *done*?'

There was complete silence. Then Ma began to cry.

Ashu and Mira had never seen Ma like that. She stayed in the living room all night, turning on the TV and alternately throwing the remote. No matter how much she watched it though, there was never anything more on the news. In fact, even the yellow line stopped running after a little while and was replaced entirely by late night shows advertising weight-loss items.

At some point, Ma took Ashu and Mira into her arms and hugged them, uncharacteristically tender in her force. Ashu listened as she asked Mira repeatedly. 'Did he do anything to you? Tell me.' Then she changed her tone. 'I promise, Mira. I won't be mad.'

Ma turned to Ashu and said, 'You, too, please.' Her voice broke.

Ashu saw it then properly, the lines on her face, the sagging skin under her eyes. The black dot on her cheek, the tears that rolled down into the folds of her neck. Ma looked so frail.

Mira didn't take long to reveal everything. She cried and told Ma everything. In broken words, in broken language. She spoke about her birthday party. And how each subsequent time Coach had come home, Mira had stayed away from him. Ma turned white, and Ashu felt a churning in his stomach. He couldn't believe it. He had been so wrapped up in his own life that he hadn't even noticed that his sister, who told him her every thought, was hiding something like this. Where was Ashu at that birthday party? With Avni and Rahul? Making fun of Mira? And how many times had Coach come around after that? Ashu wanted to cry, but seeing Ma's face—and Mira's—he tried to hold himself together.

'I'm so sorry,' Ma held Mira and stroked her hair. Mira was crying too. As Ashu looked on, he wondered if somehow, in a twisted way, the blame for this would fall on him.

But just a moment later, Ma hugged him tightly. 'I'm sorry,' she said into his ear, and though it was barely a whisper, Ashu knew what he had heard and he hugged Ma back.

That night, the three of them fell asleep together on the sofa. Ma was in the centre, and though she drifted off hugging Mira, she also had one hand wrapped around Ashu's forearm. When Ashu got up in the middle of the night, his arm throbbing with pain, he saw that Ma was now awake; she was looking at the wall with a strange expression, one Ashu hadn't seen on her face before. Was it fear? Ashu was tempted to say something to her, to offer to make her a cup of tea or to distract her—maybe tell her about where he had gone that night. But he stayed still, breathing quietly, floating in and out of a cloud of dreamless sleep, until he heard birdsong.

FLAIL

ASHU

A month passed. Summer had ripened like a peach and was now soft, quivering to burst into a new form, full of a sweetness that wasn't for everyone. People on the road covered their eyes with the canopy of their bladed fingers. Colours bled through white cotton shirts in the wash. Backs were damp with sweat. Through the patchy glass window above Ma's bed, Ashu could see himself and Mira and Ma as they moved around each other in circles. There were some days when they avoided one another, and other days when they would be coiled together, protective, each glued to the other's side.

It wasn't easy to repair the damage. There had always been a sense of unease in the house, of secrets untold and hidden, lingering in the air. But now that the can had split open, Ashu could see that there was no going back.

Ma had been with bad men before—like the man with the leather shoes who had taught Ashu how to drive when he was only eight or the one who called Ma big and fat (yet made her feel small). Some of them had been unremarkable, boring, and Ashu would wonder why she was with them. But never before had Ma been like this—untethered, like she had forgotten who she was—at the end of a relationship. Maybe something had changed within them all.

Ashu knew he was affected too. Moments came to him in snatches—how close Coach stood sometimes when he spoke to him, the way his breath smelled, the way he put his arm around Mira. How she avoided sitting next to him when he came home. Ashu shuddered when he remembered that. He wanted to throw up.

When the phone rang at home these days, Ashu imagined what would happen if it was Rahul on the other end. What would Ashu say to him if they spoke again? Ashu wasn't the best with words, but years of living with Ma had taught him that it didn't take too much to hurt someone. All he had to do was call Rahul spineless, scared, unpopular. If Rahul appeared thick-skinned and unfazed by this, Ashu would only have to push harder, shout at him, raise his voice higher than he ever had before, tell him Rahul was just like his dad. That he, too, would grow up and drink too much, be unhappy his whole life and make everybody else miserable too.

But when it came to it, he would never say those things. Because the truth was that Ashu didn't hate Rahul. His care for him wasn't a plant that had died from neglect. Instead it had now bloomed into something larger than itself, something Ashu could barely fathom, let alone take care of, but he could see seedlings of new feelings sprouting up alongside it: loneliness, fear, confusion, shame.

'You should just kiss someone else in front of him,' Avni said to him over the phone when Ashu called her one late evening. 'That will do the trick.'

Ashu laughed. He was never going to take her advice, but it was reassuring to have someone else look at his situation and not think that it was the worst thing in the world. The levity of her voice reminded him of the brief period of sunshine in his summer. When the mangoes burst open and rolled over from the trees. When there was possibility in the air and anything could happen.

Still, life at school—Ashu had been packed off after his arm had healed—was normal now. There was a satisfaction, however brief and tense, in knowing that he had done his best. He had left his heart out and someone had taken it, however briefly. He had always wondered, when he was younger, about love. He tried to find answers in the movies he watched, noticed Ma's boyfriends, tried to decipher why people fell in love, how they did it and why they stopped. But now, Ashu felt that maybe people didn't ever fall out of love. Perhaps love fell out of them. Maybe they gave so much, so soon, so fast, that the love went gushing out like blood from an oozing elbow—and then stopped.

Most of the time, Ashu only saw Rahul on the fringes. The back of his head bent over his notebook in class. A blur of tanned ankles as he rushed past Ashu on the dull grass of the football field. His narrow fingers as they crushed together leaves after smoking a cigarette with the rest of the boys. But never his tiger stripes, never his back.

Ashu was tempted sometimes to just get up and go to Ma and tell her he had kissed a boy. He wondered if she would understand. He wasn't sure, but he savoured the imminent pleasure of mouthing the words and, for once, seeing Ma's face getting filled with horror.

But Ma was different these days. Ashu could often hear her late at night, long after Mira had fallen asleep, crying, howling the way Mira sometimes did when her toe got stubbed by a door. It was relentless. Ashu thought that he should do something. For the first time in their relationship, he felt like *he* could be the one deciding if he wanted to give love. It was a powerful and heady sensation, and Ashu didn't know what to do with it, so he didn't do anything at all.

Ma was kinder to him now. She said less. She often lapsed into thought. Almost raised her voice, but quietened down, like she realised she couldn't do that anymore. Sometimes, she stopped mid-speech. In the middle of walking, she paused. She sat with Mira and Ashu a lot more, spoke to both of them, gave them each a hug. Some days, even when Mira wasn't around, she sat next to Ashu, made him place his head on her lap, asked about his day. Ma loved him, Ashu knew. She had just taken a long while to show it. And even though it was hard to most times, he loved her back.

In the meantime, the trees kept growing thick and profuse. Ashu could see wildflowers emerging, big, unruly shrubs, and animals, large crows and bats, rattlesnakes and dandelions, an entire ecosystem of his loneliness enveloping him. All he could do in that moment was to sit down so his knees didn't buckle and wait, breathe and wait. And one by one, the trees would ungrow and turn to soil, the bats would disappear in pitch black air and the shrubs would return to earth.

The only difference was that Ashu no longer questioned why he felt that way. It was deep inside his skin, part of who he was.

* * *

Ashu was pleasantly surprised when Ma opened her cupboard to take out a photo album. It was the first time she had chosen to show Ashu and Mira their baby pictures. The photographs were dusty and grey and beautiful. There were admittedly few of Ashu alone, but he didn't mind so much. He loved seeing pictures of them as a normal family. He loved seeing his own face squished up against Mira's, seeing Ma when she was younger, seeing his father. Mira was only a baby in the photographs, so she didn't look like much of anything but a lump of rice. Ashu felt happy that even at just five, he'd already started looking so much like his father.

At the end of the evening, Ma asked Ashu to put the album back. As he rummaged through the crowded shelves for space, he heard a heavy thud. The album had fallen to the floor, along with a dusty red book. He flipped through its pages and saw it was a journal, scrawled with a handwriting he knew as well as his own bones. Feeling a swell of curiosity rise in him, he placed one book back in the cupboard and carried the other to his room.

There was something thrilling, Ashu discovered over the next few days, about living in someone else's head. It was a welcome break from his own life, a distraction from everything that had fallen apart over the summer. He kept Ma's journal in the drawer by his bed, in the same place he hid cigarette singles and spare change, all of which he dipped into whenever he got the chance.

Ashu wasn't one to read. Ma had tried to get him into the habit, and as was her way, resented him for not taking to it. It was as though not being literary was a character fault and amounted to him being a bad person.

But this wasn't any boring old book. It was the story of Ma.

Ashu knew what he was doing was wrong—it was like rifling through someone else's dreams. But once he'd started turning the pages, he couldn't stop. He sat in the dark, chin propped by his hands, and read snatches of Ma's life. He read it slow, then read it fast, read it before meals and after class; when Mira was out of the house, when Ma was away.

It was fun to read stories of Ma's childhood. He thought he recognised some of the people in her journal entries. Faces, both old and unfamiliar formed and dissolved in his mind simultaneously, like tiny ripples in still water. He laughed at his grandmother and the story about god in a plate of idli and vada. He thought he would have liked her. He was surprised to read about what Ma was like at school. But the real thrill began when his own name started to pepper the pages. Ma had never told Ashu anything of consequence from his childhood. He yearned to know where they used to live, what his first words were, what his father had been like, and why Ma had kept it all hidden. But the deeper Ashu fell into the story, the more he realised that there was nothing enjoyable about it. This was a dark cave that he had entered without a flashlight, and there was no going back.

Ashu lowered the journal to his lap. His hands trembled. A shadow crisscrossed his face, forming a cage of light and dark. There was a pit at the bottom of his stomach, and the more Ashu thought about what he had just read, the deeper the pit sank. He darted to the basin and could barely lock the bathroom door before he began throwing up. He felt much like he did when he had heard the news about Coach.

After washing his face with water, he sat still on his bed for a few minutes; he thought about what to do. When he decided, his eyes hardened, they were like the marbles he had found with a friend once on a warm terrace floor. He could hear Ma and Mira reading aloud from a storybook in the living room and laughing.

Ashu walked into Ma's room, and like he had a few months ago, lifted her mattress and found some money underneath. Then, he placed the red journal on her bed and walked out. He didn't look at the small window above the cupboard. He didn't look at the sky outside.

In the living room, as he reached for the front door, Ma turned to him and called out, 'Where are you going, Ashu?'

'Out.' He stared at the ground.

'To the market?' said Ma. 'Can you get some chillies?'

He nodded, stuffing his hands deeper into his pocket.

'Ashu?' Mira scrambled from Ma's lap and appeared at his side. 'Can I come too?' she asked, widening her big eyes at him.

Ashu shook his head. 'Nah. Not this time,' he said and kissed her cheek.

His knees trembled. He shut the door behind him and exhaled.

Outside, the sky looked like it was on fire. The small tangerine flowers on the tree across the yard were in bloom for one last time that season, then the tree would be bare. Ashu heard a sharp sound and looked up to see a crow sitting on a branch, cawing loudly. He kept walking, out of the house, towards the road, farther and farther away from home, straight into the bright orange sun.

It happened a few weeks after my husband died. It had been raining all night. The house was in disarray, the sink piling up with dirty dishes and empty cardboard boxes open everywhere. I had hardly slept in days. For the second time in my life, I had been attacked by grief. But unlike when my mother died, this grief wasn't quiet. It didn't sneak in on me unannounced or quietly settle into my skin. No. This time, the grief was obnoxious. It had flooded over me even before he had really gone.

My husband came into my life at a time when I needed him, and he changed the way I thought about the world. Because of him, I began to trust family. I gave up on some of the best years of my life. I became a mother, a wife. I stayed home. For him. My thoughts oscillated. Going from wistful and beautiful—to angry. So angry. Yes, that was what was different about my grief this time.

It had been raining since the morning, not abating for a moment all day. I idly imagined what would happen if it never stopped. Would all of Delhi flood over, taking the three of us along? What would happen the next day if, when the sun was supposed to rise, it simply decided not to and the sky remained black? Would we all stay indoors forever, or would we learn to live, work, breathe in the dark like in one of those Nordic countries where no one ever smiles and everyone wears thermals all the time? The thought made me smile.

I sat up that night with a cup of tea and watched the thunderstorm. Mira was fast asleep in my room. She was the only one who would never really know what had happened with her father. But maybe, she had sensed that something was wrong. She was sick a lot, was sleeping far less than babies her age were supposed to. I, too, was having a hard time. Still, her presence was comforting to me. I started making her sleep right next to me in bed, where my husband used to. Mira would grab my finger with her chubby hands and make me feel less lonely.

That night though, even Mira couldn't comfort me. I was riled up, angry. The storm didn't help. I walked to the kitchen to make myself something to eat—something that wasn't for my husband or Ashu or Mira—but I failed. There were the sweet potatoes that my husband liked and Mira's baby food on the counter. Ashu only liked to eat bananas at the time, and I had stocked up the kitchen with them. I looked through drawers, inside the cupboard. There wasn't a single thing that I would've wanted to eat, not a single thing that was mine. Suddenly, I studied the house and saw how everything was owned by my husband, or there were things I had bought, but only because he said that he liked them. What was for me?

As I rummaged, I found some alcohol under the sink. Neither of us drank very much. Drinking made my husband feel queasy. I didn't really drink either because unlike some women, I didn't need alcohol to sleep with my husband. Still, this was a bottle of whiskey he had once been gifted by his boss. It was cheap, I could tell from the sticker peeling off. I got a glass, then abruptly put it away. Bringing the bottle to my lips, I felt the bitter liquid flow through my chest and let it burn.

Later, I found myself in Ashu's room. It must have been one or two in the morning. The thunder was loud, a whip lashing across the sky. This was a downpour like I'd never seen before. The clouds were grieving too. It was shocking to me that my children could sleep through something like this. But there he was, Ashu, lying on his side, his knees tucked into his chest like he had been about to hug them but fell asleep before he could. There was drool on his pillow—an ugly little patch of saliva that had slipped from his mouth.

I stared at him, at the nose curving at his forehead, his skin moist with sweat. He was sleeping peacefully. My vision turned blurry the more I stared at him. He looked to me like the man who had once pushed me into the car seat and muffled my voice. For a second, he even looked like my husband. But it thundered again, and Ashu went back to looking like himself. No matter how long I stared though, he never looked like me.

Did he know? The pain he had caused? The place he came from? Even in my husband's final moments, Ashu had entered my dreams uninvited and stopped me from waking up. Who knows what might have happened if I had awakened in time?

I walked closer to Ashu, knelt beside the bed. I must have looked like I was in prayer. I traced my fingers across his forehead, over his nose. He turned to his other side, and for a second, he looked like an angel. I could love him, I remember thinking from that last dream. I could. But again, thunder struck, and I picked up a pillow. I brought it closer to his face. Two minutes. Two minutes is all it would take.

He began squirming underneath. I stayed silent, just pushed the pillow in further. But then, I caught a glimpse of myself against the bedroom window, eyes savage, hair all over the place. I couldn't recognise myself.

I was shaking by the time I realised what I was doing.

I lifted the pillow and let go.

Soon, I packed up both the kids and went to another city where no one would follow us. It was small, nothing compared to Delhi, but I just wanted to get away. I sold the tiniest pieces of jewellery that my mother had left for me, took the money I had stashed away, lost touch with family. My husband had saved some money too—most of it had gone towards treating him, but the little that was left got us by for the first year or two.

I had to leave quickly before Mira and Ashu could ask too many questions. I often wished I could be like them. That with the march of time, I, too, could lose my memory. The parts that hurt, the parts that were happy. That I had someone bigger than me, stronger than me, who could edit my history. That I, too, could put a soft blanket over my face and wake up the next day, the past more distant than ever.

For years, no one was in touch with me, and I was in touch with no one. My sister tried to wriggle her way into my life. I heard rumours that her marriage was collapsing. But I couldn't help her. I could barely help myself. Besides, it was too late. I had Mira, I had Ashu, I had a job and I had a life, whatever you could make of it. In the past few years, I had moved from a flat with my parents to a house with my husband and back to a tiny flat, now with the kids, my living spaces shrinking and expanding like the bellows of a harmonium, squeezing me and my belongings with them.

When I met Anita, I made her place in my life clear from the start. I was a friend, a good friend, but could never be the closest one. I could ask her for help with Mira and Ashu sometimes, and she could say no if she wanted to. She never did. We could talk about books, films, our colleagues at work, our boss. Any chitchat about the past and any form of advice—those were off limits. I guess the rules worked for her. She must have been lonely.

I thought about my mother a lot in those early days after my husband's death. I pictured what would have happened if she were alive. Would she finally have seen me because I was a mother of two—would that have been the thing to connect us, even repair us? Would she have judged me for the choices I had made to get myself here? Or would she have still gone ahead and picked my sister over me, because my sister hadn't been irresponsible and lost her husband, and everyone knew that an alive husband, however useless, was still better than a dead one?

Sometimes I wonder what life would have been like if I hadn't gone on that date. If I hadn't borrowed a denim skirt, if I had worn jeans instead. I wouldn't have had Ashu, maybe I wouldn't even have had Mira. Perhaps I really would have gone on to pursue a postgraduate degree, fallen in love with a new city and stayed there. Maybe I would've never gotten married at all. For years, I fantasised about these things, thought about them in brief moments between picking the kids up from school and dropping them off, between reaching work and turning off the car's engine.

For a few years, I stopped seeing men. Everyone reminded me of my husband. Of the intensity in his gaze, his knitted eyebrows, his calf muscles when he flexed them, of the way he was particular about his CD collection. No one ever matched him, and it was disappointing, insulting even, to try to replace him.

Sometimes, I saw in Ashu glimpses of the man I'd once been with, shadows in his personality, and I tried to clamp them down. Slowly, over time, Ashu became more reserved, quieter, more obedient. I was satisfied.

There were times that I got lonely. But I read. I made up games with the kids, I cooked up rules, and time passed. Then, I started dating again. Sometimes, it wasn't a good idea. Most of the men weren't. Still, they were adults who could hold adult conversation. None of them lasted for too long. Not long enough for me to develop strong feelings.

I had successfully managed to deep clean my life, purge it of its past. All that had happened had even stopped appearing in my dreams. Then, one day, when the kids were still young, the ceiling exploded with water and flooded the house. I was frustrated. I began cleaning everything out. The cupboard by the table, a closet that we hardly ever used. I tugged the handle open and things, many things—a rickety old globe, clothes, encyclopaedias and an old garbage bag—tumbled down. I realised that the garbage bag was the only thing I'd really carried here with me from Delhi. In it were bits and bobs from my old life. Silver jewellery pieces, Mira's first pair of studs, books, yellowed, withering. Some of Mira's baby clothes. Once or twice, as I rummaged through the pile, I thought that I saw my husband's socks or his ties, an old bottle of his cologne—but it couldn't have been. I was sure I had thrown it all away.

Eventually as I dug, I saw something dull, familiar, as though from a recurring dream. I picked it up and sat down on my bed. It was a journal given to me once by my mother, on my lap now like a weighted stone. All of a sudden, the smell of agarbatti, the fluttering of wings, the cool touch of my husband's hand came to me. Simon & Garfunkel, camphor, the sound of a TV, a phone call. Soon, I was crying tears I had not shed before. I needed time, so I put a chair against my bedroom door to lock my room. I ignored the kids when they called out to me. Ashu was still just seven or eight. Mira was three. I suppose I didn't realise when I had fallen asleep. I woke up later at night, parched, confused. I began throwing each object back into the bag, leaving only one thing behind. I shoved the bag back in the cupboard. I sat on the damp floor. I opened the journal. I began to write.

BREATHE

MIRA

It's been almost six-seven-eight months since I turned nine, but Ma still acts like I'm five and will be forever. She kisses me loudly on my ear, even outside school where people like Misi and Lina can see. And though it feels nice and all, to have Ma in a good mood and hug me so tight that my stomach goes grrrrr and she says, 'Aren't you a hungry lil monster?' right inside my ear, it's a bit embarrassing now that I'm nine.

Ma is quite bored nowadays. She waits for me outside school when the day is done. She drops me right by the classroom in the morning and holds my hand till I tug and tug and the school bell rings and I have to go. At night also, when we go to bed, she makes me sleep right next to her even though I can't sleep when she snores like a big bear and I want to say Maa! Stop!

And if I by mistake fall asleep in my own bed, in the morning, I find Ma crawled into bed with me. Even though she sometimes squishes my fingers, I snuggle up closer to her to smell her hair, close my eyes and sleep some more.

* * *

When Ashu left, Ma thought we had lost him. Like he was a pair of socks or your homework when you don't feel like doing it. Lost. We looked for him everywhere—we went to the school, we went to Rahul's place, we checked with all the neighbours but they gave us funny looks. Finally, we even went to the police station, which Ma hated. A big man with baggy brown trousers and a black belt kept licking his lips and looking at me and Ma. We had to tell him three times what had happened, and only then did he start writing with his pen, but really, I don't think he wrote anything at all. Finally, Ma got a call at home the next day.

'Is it Ashu?' I asked. I pulled on her arm to make her give the phone to me, but she didn't. She asked the person on the phone a couple more questions and put down the receiver. 'He's fine.' She looked at me. 'Your brother's safe.'

When my new friends at school ask me about who's in my family, I say there are two of us right now, but once, there were three, and even before that, a long, long time ago, there were four. They look at me with big eyes and get confused. What! they say. And I try to explain. I want Misi and Lina to understand that Ashu is a nice brother—the best brother in the world. I tell them that he had a big fight with Ma for Godknowswhat, and now he's gone to stay with our Mausi. He's happier there. Delhi's a big city, and no one really cares if Ashu holds a boy's hand like I once saw him hold Rahul's. Ashu still doesn't know I know this, but once, Ashu and Rahul were sitting very close to each other and looking into each other's eyes like people on TV right before they're about to kiss. The second I entered the room, they jumped apart and pretended they were reading a book. I didn't say anything, but come on, people. I'm nine, not five. I know that Ashu doesn't just *read* for fun.

* * *

Avni called and said that Ashu is my half-brother and I'm his half-sister. Half! she repeated. She sounded like she were laughing through the phone. I told her that she was a Full Idiot and hung up.

Later, when I asked, Ma wouldn't explain what Avni meant. She didn't even ask me to look it up in the dictionary, which she usually does. She just kept saying Not Now or Later, but really, I know that means Never.

* * *

We went to the dentist's again, me and Ma. Her teeth have been paining, so the doctor made her open her mouth wide. He put a big torchlight into her mouth so Ma's teeth shone like rocks in the rain. He prodded with metal spoons and knives. Then he put his arms down and said, 'Nothing.' Ma said that dentist was a fool and went to the chemist and bought medicine anyway.

Later, I sat down on her lap to put gum paint on her. Her mouth smelt a little, and I took my tiny finger and spread the medicine all over her gum, just me, all by myself. Ma pretended to close her mouth and eat my fingers like they were cold carrot sticks. We played the game four-five times, and by the end of it, Ma's gum paint was all over my hand, and we were both laughing and laughing and laughing like we hadn't in days.

On days like this, I forget that everything has changed. I think that I'll walk back into our room and see Ashu. He'll be sitting on the bed and bouncing a ball off the wall. And I'll sit on the top of the bunk bed, and he'll say Mira, get off!

But when I realise that he isn't there, I call him up at Mausi's house, and we talk. Sometimes, for a long time. We laugh and we talk about everything, and that's easy now because there are no more secrets inside any of us, and we know everything about each other. I tell him all the things that happened at school, and he tells me about the new people he's meeting. I tell him what I ate, and he tells me what he drank. I can tell if he is shuffling his feet or holding his breath or secretly letting out farts, because I know him best, much better than Avni, even if he's my half-brother or full-brother or any kind of brother at all. When we are on the phone, he sounds as if he is right here in the room, and there's no one else. No Ma, No Avni, No Mausi listening. Just me and Ashu talking to each other, like it used to be, and making funny sounds and laughing till someone makes him keep down the phone and we stop.

But some days, like today, Ashu is quiet and distracted. I call him up, but he doesn't really talk. He acts like a ghost.

Me: Hellooo, Ashu!

Ashu: Hi, silly

Me: When are you coming home?

Ashu: —

Me: Tomorrow? Next week?

Ashu: —

Me: Next month?

Ashu: —

This time, he's the one giving me the Silent Treatment, but honestly, I don't know what to do. Some days, Ashu doesn't pick up my phone at all. It rings, but no one answers. Ma says he must be too busy. Misi and Lina say that I should just come play with them and forget about it. But really, it's okay. I don't mind. I'll just keep on calling and calling and calling.

ACKNOWLEDGEMENTS

I have many people to thank for supporting me throughout the making of my debut novel *Hot Water.*

Thank you so much to the wonderful team at Jacaranda Books for publishing this book—Afua Ofori-Darko, Valerie Brandes, Magdalene Abraha, Zain Kazerooni and everyone else on the team. Thank you to Christina Schweighardt for this beautiful cover. My sincerest gratitude to the luminous Sareeta Domingo, who saw light in the story, and commissioned it. I am honoured to be part of Sareeta's List and her legacy, and wish I could have gotten to know her better.

Thank you to Carla Briner for her invaluable feedback, relentless drive and bright smile. A huge thank you to Anna Soler-Pont, Clara Rosell, Carol and everyone at Pontas Film & Literary Agency.

Many thanks to my publishers at HarperCollins in India for first publishing this book: Rahul Soni, Dharini Bhaskar, and Ananth Padmanabhan.

Thank you to JJ Bola for the warm support, our meeting at Foyles and for sharing advice that one could never find in the books. Thank you also to Maria Cardona-Serra for selecting my manuscript for the novel-in-progress prize.

I am grateful to all my teachers and workshop facilitators for being generous with their craft—including Tanushree Dey, Rakhi Roy, Miriam Gamble, Jane McKie, Jane Alexander, Allyson Stack and Joyati Sen.

I am deeply thankful to the authors Deepa Anappara, Aravind Jayan, Iqbal Husain, Onyi Nwabineli, JJ Bola and Amrita Mahale who have carved out the time to endorse this novel.

My writing workshop friends—Alexandra Ye, Amos O'Connor, Erin Howell, Fan Du, Alice Rogers—thank you for the invaluable feedback and constant encouragement. Thank you to all my other writer friends too, including Alex Penland, Alycia Pirmohamed, Anthi Cheimariou, Apoorva Dutt, Dean Atta, Heather Parry, Hemant Kumar, Selali Fiamanya and Xaviere Musih-Tejdi, and all those I've met this year.

A special thank you to my friend Athul Prasad for taking my author portraits. Thank you to Aman Deshmukh for our conversations about the creative life. A huge thank you to my friends, Vamika and Jayati, for your love and for reading early parts of drafts; and to my friends Roopika, Nupur, Aditi, Prerna, for your support.

To Juno, the sweetest puppy, who had a brief but unforgettable life.

I'm forever grateful to my big and extended family, who have been my greatest cheerleaders. My deepest gratitude to all my grandparents. Thank you to my nieces and nephews for being endless sources of inspiration, including baby Vir. A special thank you to Rakesh Govil and Neeta Govil for all their love. Thank you to Namrata and Akshat. Thank you to Ruchira Mittal, Putta Didi and Chetan Jija for their support and infectious energy.

To my parents, Sunita Govil and Vijay Kumar Govil, who are uniquely positive and wonderful souls—and in my opinion, the most loving parents in the world. Thank you so much.

To my brother-in-law, Abhinav Mehra, thank you for becoming such a pivotal member of our lives and for always asking me with a cheeky grin, 'Book done, Bhaviks?' Thank you to my sister, Laksheeta Govil for believing in me. My first reader and the best friend a girl could ever have. Experiencing childhood with you, and growing up together has been a joy.

Thank you to Yajur Mittal, my husband, for standing by me and fueling me with your positive energy and encouragement. You are the best example of love in this novel and in life. The one with the tiger stripes; the one who gently smoothens down the snags of my thumb.

ABOUT THE AUTHOR

Photo credit: Athul Prasad

Bhavika Govil is a writer from New Delhi who dreams of the sea. Her short fiction has appeared in *Granta* and *Wasafiri*, and has been shortlisted for the ALCS Tom-Gallon Trust Award and the Queen Mary Wasafiri New Writing Prize. She holds a master's degree in creative writing from the University of Edinburgh and teaches writing workshops.

Hot Water is her debut novel. First published in India by Fourth Estate, HarperCollins, it was shortlisted for the Godrej Literature Live! First Book Award and appeared on national bestseller lists. An extract won the Pontas & JJ Bola Emerging Writers Prize. The novel is being translated into other languages.